MW00860692

ISBN: 9781942857747

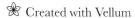 Created with Vellum

Enthrall

THE FREED BILLIONAIRE
SPENCER CHRISTMAS TRILOGY
BOOK ONE

Z.L. ARKADIE

Sweat trickles into both my eyes, and I squeeze them shut until the stinging subsides. I can't stop now. I want to stop, but I can't. The sound of metal banging against concrete crashes throughout the dank hallway. I can't get her out of my mind—Jada Forte.

Impulse is taking over. I could feel it energizing my hands, my brain telling me to drop my power tool and *go see her right now*. I take a deep breath, and after forcing the air out of my lungs, I obey. What I'm about to do flies in the face of reason. Remorse impedes my steps.

Don't go, Spencer.

I have to.

I must see her, watch her.

I clutch my heavy heart as one entrance leads to the next, and then the next. Soon, I'm in Jada's room, walking down the hallway. My steps are virtually silent. I could hear her breathing while sleeping. My conscience issues me a final warning, *don't do it*. It's too late. I'm now standing at her bedside, wondering, what's so special about this one? Why am I having this kind of reaction to her?

CHAPTER ONE

JADA FORTE

I was spent, my skin was sticky, and I smelled like a landfill. I was on my third day without a shower, but fortunately, I was on the brink of reaching my final destination. My tired eyes stared out the window from the back seat of my new billionaire boss's hired car as I tried to keep up with the alien environment we were passing through. My eyelids were becoming heavier by the second. Thank goodness my driver had already signaled that he didn't want to engage in small talk by grunting incoherently when I asked him how far away the ranch was from the airport. Normally, I would have pushed for some sort of reassuring answer. But I was way too exhausted to do that.

All I could see through my weary eyes were tall

evergreens hugging the edges of both sides of the road, which every now and then gave way to sprawling fields of wild grass. A mountain range, purpling from the setting sun, stretched across the horizon under a sky filled with ominous clouds. I could tell it had been raining a lot in this part of the country lately, even though I was only a recent arrival. Everything was damp—the road, the blades of grass, the leaves, and even the air. One thing was for sure—I was no longer in Manhattan.

I'd been scheduled to arrive in Jackson Hole, Wyoming, on Monday, and it was already Wednesday. Three days before, while I was on a layover in Salt Lake City, a fire had ignited in one of the terminals, and because of that, all flights going out had ground to a halt until an investigation could be completed. The ordeal put me in a perilous position. I was flying on standby and only had six dollars in my wallet and a hundred thirty-three dollars in my bank account, which I couldn't touch because the minimum payment on one of my maxed-out credit cards was due, and I needed the funds to stay in my account to cover it.

Whereas most other travelers were able to successfully reschedule their flights, I had to wait on standby for a seat to become available. By the last flight of the day, I still hadn't gotten a seat, which forced me to sleep in uncomfortable airport chairs. After the first night, I was tempted to call my mother, Congresswoman Patricia Forte, and ask for help, but dealing with her was like making a deal with Rumpelstiltskin. She'd want not only my first-born to control forever but my whole generation as well. I couldn't ask my dad, either, because it seemed he had been under her thumb since the day they tied the knot. Everything I said to him always got back to her. I could wait it out another day and forgo sleep another night or call my new employer, a billionaire named Spencer Christmas, and ask for help. My third option was the one I almost succumbed to, and that was to say "Screw Wyoming," head back to New York, and take my best friend, Hope, up on her offer to move in with her until I could find a job in the city.

But the pay… oh, the pay…

I hadn't had a steady salary since a major media company absorbed Caldwell Jamison, the PR firm I used to work for, and my position was deemed redundant. I was let go in January and had been living off bountiful savings since then. Even though I hadn't been wasteful, only spending money on bills, groceries, and other essentials a girl needed, I was now broke—like, scraping-the-bottom-of-the-barrel broke.

I had come across a job listing from Spencer Christmas of the Christmas Family Industry Holdings months before. Even though it was for an assistant, the pay—five thousand dollars a week—was substantially more than my previous job. I was so surprised by the amount that I checked to make sure I hadn't accidentally found my way to a phishing site. I hadn't. The listing was on the official Headhunters Deluxe website, and it was one of those that was only shown to a handful of candidates who had special keywords in their résumés that enticed the employer.

The Christmases' name was in the same category as DuPont, Carnegie, and Rockefeller. If anyone could afford to pay an assistant that much money, it would be someone with the last name of Christmas. So I clicked the apply button. I never expected to hear back from anyone, but on Friday, I received a call.

"Is this Jada Forte?" the man asked in a lifeless tone of voice.

I felt my forehead wrinkle. "It is, and to whom am I speaking?" I asked, remembering to sound professional. A job interview could come at any moment, and I wanted to always sound capable to a prospective employer.

"This is Spencer Christmas. I find your experience valuable. Could you start in three days?"

I pursed my lips, thinking. I didn't know much about the Christmases other than that the patriarch, who had been dead for some time, was a pervert. I also knew that the brothers were hot—like, JFK Jr. hot—and rich and probably too damn important to make hiring calls to potential assistants.

"Is this Hope screwing with me?" I asked.

He remained silent for a beat. "I am not Hope, and I am not screwing with you."

My muscles tensed, and a flare of adrenaline fired up my brain. "Are you really Spencer Christmas?" I asked, clutching my suddenly queasy stomach as I recalled how much the job paid.

"Yes," he said curtly.

"I'm sorry, but it's hard for me to believe you would make this sort of call yourself."

"I understand," he whispered. "This job requires a sizeable amount of discretion. You will be working for me personally, not for my company. I've read your résumé and checked your background. As I said, I would like to hire you for this job."

I felt the tension in my body deflate. He had effectively put my mind at ease. *Holy shit*, I thought. I was on the phone with an actual billionaire. "Yes, I'm sorry, but is the salary really five K a week?"

"Yes," he said in the same monotone voice.

I opened my mouth, silently screaming as a thrill raced through me, even though I knew my mom would not be pleased with me taking an assistant job no matter how much it paid. I could hear her lecturing me. "Jada, why would you make the asinine decision of taking a professional position that's so beneath you? An assistant? This will ruin your upward trajectory. Wrong." I pictured her shaking her head at how pathetic my decision made me. "So very wrong."

But fuck pleasing my mom—in one month, I would be able to pay off all my overextended credit cards and save up again for another rainy day. I wouldn't be under so much pressure to find just any job, and I could make the perfect career choice for me.

"Yes, sure. I'll take the job," I said, masking my excitement.

"Fine. Are you able to relocate?"

My happiness fizzled into distress. "Relocate?"

"To Jackson Hole, Wyoming," he said as if he

had no idea what sort of bombshell he had just dropped on me.

I chewed on my bottom lip, trying to picture the distance between Manhattan and somewhere in Wyoming called Jackson Hole. *Hole?*

His silence lingered for longer than I would have expected, as if he knew I needed time to process the news. Perhaps that was why the pay was so hefty. Who in their right mind would leave a city like Manhattan for a city with "Hole" in the name?

My friends were in New York. Not only that, but I would miss the steam rising out of the street, the people driving as if their vehicles were gladiators battling in an arena, and skyscrapers of all shapes, sizes, and ages and used for a million purposes. We could take our pick—eat here, shop there, pawn our shit, bank, peruse, fuck, you name it—on any New York City boulevard. So when my first answer came to me, it was definite.

"Sorry, sir, but…"

"Ten thousand a week," he said as if we were in the middle of a fierce negotiation.

I nearly knocked my lukewarm coffee off my desk and had to close my mouth to swallow before speaking again. "I'm sorry, did you say ten thousand a week?" I coughed to clear my throat.

"And I need a commitment of six months," he added.

My brain did the math. I would make nearly a quarter of a million dollars. "Wait, six months at ten thousand dollars a week?" I asked, needing to hear him answer in the affirmative with the two factors put in the same sentence.

"Yes, that's correct."

There was no need for him to repeat it or to sweeten the deal. I had acquiesced.

Initially, he was going to fly me to Wyoming, but he called me back an hour later to mumble that the account he'd been planning to use wouldn't work. He asked if I could find my way to the ranch, saying he would reimburse me upon arrival. Again, there was no way I wanted to let a man as rich as Spencer Christmas know how broke I was and that I was taking the job he was offering out of desperation.

"Sure, no problem," I said like a person who already had two hundred forty thousand in her bank account.

With my last two hundred bucks of disposable cash in the bank, I bought a standby ticket for $191. Hope drove me to the airport, so I didn't have to pay to ride the subway. Luckily, I was able to get a fast flight out of New York and didn't hit a snag until Salt Lake City.

On night one of my delay, I came close to getting a flight, but the late party showed up at the last minute, and I was bumped from the only available seat on the small airplane. I ended up trying to sleep while lying across three very uncomfortable chairs. The next day, I was bumped from every flight that was heading to Jackson Hole. The ticket agents kept apologizing, promising that what was happening was unprecedented.

By night two, everyone who worked behind the counter was pulling for me to hook a flight and not get bumped. After having to sleep on those uncomfortable seats again, I was forced to choose option number two and call Spencer Christmas to ask for help.

I frantically relayed my experience of the last forty-eight hours. Once I finished gushing, I squeezed my eyes shut and took a breath. He remained as silent as a church mouse for way too long.

"Hello?" I finally asked.

"You're in Salt Lake City," he said in the same lackluster tone he'd used when he offered me the job.

"Um, yes," I replied, half hoping he would just fire me.

"I'll call you back." He hung up.

The chilling remnants of his voice haunted me. There was something certainly wrong with a man who had no variation in his tone. I was a sensitive person, and I could feel his unhappiness seeping into my mind and infecting my soul. I twisted my neck to ease the soreness, which came from lying on the seats, and kept shifting as I sat, trying to get comfortable. I'd already felt a little jittery about taking the job, but after that conversation, I was having serious doubts.

Just come back home where you belong, I heard my mother's voice say.

But where is that? New York or California? I asked the Patricia who resided in my mind.

With me, she snapped, and I quickly stiffened.

Thank goodness my phone rang again. It was Mr. Christmas, and he said a car would be waiting for me at Arrivals within an hour. He ended the call in the same abrupt manner he'd used earlier.

"Wow, what a…" I whispered, looking at my phone. I didn't want to say it. If he turned out to be an asshole, that would be the worse-case scenario— no one wanted to pack up, talk her landlord into allowing her to vacate her apartment without notice, accept her friend's offer to pick up her things and put them in storage, and travel to some place she'd never heard of, all to work for an abominable asshole.

It took nearly an hour to get my luggage from the standby area. I was sweaty with every step, feeling as if my feet were made of cement, by the time a car took me to another airport in the vicinity. This time, I boarded a small private airplane and left Salt Lake City for Jackson Hole. The flight was bumpy with no frills or thrills. I prayed the whole way and prepared to die, especially after the aircraft took a sharp dip. At twenty-nine years old, I was probably too young for a heart attack, but for a little while, I thought I was having one. Then the pilot's voice came over the loudspeaker, apologizing for the drop and telling me not to worry and that the turbulence was worse than usual. I took my inability to get a flight out of SLC for almost three days, the stress of getting my luggage, and the latest encounter with deathly turbulence as signs that greed had probably made me make the wrong decision. I should have stayed in New York.

MY PRAYERS HAD BEEN HEARD. WE LANDED SAFELY, and a fancy car was waiting near where the aircraft parked to take me to my destination. Each step I took made me dizzy, and I just wanted to pass out and sleep for at least a week. But now I was sitting in the back seat of a comfortable car, struggling to keep my eyes open as the vehicle approached a massive iron security gate that looked more like it belonged to a prison than to a rich family's ranch. The barrier rolled open before the driver had a chance to stop and wait.

All of a sudden, I hugged myself to keep from shaking. This was all new, and even though I could hear my mother's critical voice repeating that Fortes were strong, not whimpering and weak, I wanted to get out of the car and run in the opposite direction.

As we drove past more fields of wild grass, I faintly wondered why no animals were grazing in the distance. I thought that was the purpose of a ranch—to raise livestock. There had to be a barn-yard full of horses somewhere at least. I wanted to ask the driver about it, but he'd been silent the whole ride, and I was too exhausted to talk.

Goodness gracious, I really didn't want to be here. I visualized Mr. Christmas telling me that our arrangement wasn't going to work. It had been difficult to get a solid grasp on what he looked like in person. In photos, he was tall, was in great shape, and had a fluffy but perfectly combed head of hair and the sort of mysterious, uninhibited gaze that belonged to men who had more money than God. Hope had said she'd seen him in passing once and that I was in for the surprise of my life.

"Then he's cute?" I asked.

We'd had this conversation on the previous Friday. I met her at a bar in the East Village to tell her all about the job and ask for help in getting my affairs in order.

That wicked, amused look came into her narrowed eyes. "Here, I think we should look together." She whipped out her cellphone and placed it faceup in the middle of our table as she called up photo after photo of my new boss. The clips made it abundantly clear that he was a playboy with a cocky grin and a slouchy devil-may-care posture, carrying himself as though he was the rich douchebag crown prince of the universe. And in just about every photo, his arm was around a beautiful lovestruck woman. However, I also noticed that all the pics were from over five years ago.

"You see him?" Hope asked before clicking off her display screen. "Your new boss loves the ladies."

My smile wavered as I thought about how much his tone hadn't matched the man depicted in the Internet images. "Well, let's read some of the articles," I said, tapping her phone.

"Nope. Don't read anything about him. Go into your new situation with no judgment." She cocked her head in a curious manner. "I take it you haven't read the book, have you?"

"What book?"

"Forget about it. The less about him you know, the happier you'll be in Montana."

I rolled my eyes. "Wyoming." The fact that I had to correct her irritated me. I couldn't say why—it just did.

"Right," she replied glibly and raised a finger in caution. "As I said, don't read the book. And don't worry about him either. If he wants to fuck—and I'm sure he's going to want that from someone who has your face and body... I mean your boobs..." Hope put her hands together in prayer. "If only I had been so blessed." She was now warning me with her finger again. "But for forty thousand a month, just say no—or yes, depending on how you feel. I mean, that's if..."

I was on the edge of my seat. "If what?"

She wrinkled her nose. "Jada, aren't you a virgin?"

My mouth fell open as my skin tingled. Yes, I was a virgin, but I had never told her that. As a matter of fact, I'd made up some past sexual experiences designed to convince her I wasn't a virgin. Of course, I felt horrible about lying to my best friend, but she was one of those sexually free women. I was five-eight, but she was two inches taller, so guys always saw Hope first when we walked into a room. Her light-auburn hair was baby fine, and her brown almond eyes and heart-shaped face made her as sexy as a Kardashian. So lots of men wanted to sleep with her, and she was not the sort of woman who brokered her pussy for a better deal—Hope did not need to know there was a ring in her future before she slept with a guy. I wasn't that way, either, but I was a different animal from Hope. The last thing I needed from a man was his dick inside me. The first thing I wanted from any man who would be my lover would be a sharp mind and a kind heart, but he couldn't be a pushover like my dad.

"Me, a virgin? Why would you ask that?" My tone was way too defensive not to give me away, but it was too late to change it.

She scrutinized me long enough for me to keep shifting in my seat.

"What?" I snapped.

"Well, listen, Jada. All I'll say is Spencer Christmas is not the sort of guy you hand your V-card to unless you're in it strictly for kicks. And, Jada, you're not a simply-for-kicks kind of girl. So here's my advice—if fucking is part of the deal, then let the money go."

The house was now in view. The sheer scale of it, as well as the design, made my eyes open wider. It was the size of a mansion but had the design of a luxury chateau and a craftsman-styled luxurious estate home, made mostly of wood with lots of large picture windows and tall chimneys blowing smoke into the cold atmosphere from just about every corner.

The car stopped in front of a set of steps leading to the front entrance. A shiver ran down my spine as I thought I saw the form of a tall man with an athletic frame standing deep behind the glass doors. I craned my neck and narrowed my eyes to get a better look.

"This is the end of the road, Ms. Forte," the driver said.

Suddenly, a tall white-haired man in a black suit

walked out of the house and was standing in front of the door, waiting for me. He was certainly not the person I first saw.

The driver opened my door and held it that way until I got out. I let my curious gaze dart from one large window to the next. If the person I'd seen seconds before was Spencer Christmas, he was now long gone. I smiled at the man in the suit, who was watching me with a stoical expression, and tried to convince myself that the phantom of a person who might or might not be my new boss had not made my stomach flutter.

CHAPTER TWO

JADA FORTE

I followed the driver up the walkway as he rolled my two large suitcases and carried my gigantic weekender bag with the strap slung over his shoulder. He handled them a lot more easily than I had. The air was crisp, clean, and nippy. I hugged myself to keep from shivering, which I was doing not because I was cold but because awareness had just slammed into me like a ton of bricks. I had flown across the country to live in a stranger's luxury ranch house. The job description said I would be performing normal executive assistant duties, like keeping a calendar, doing bookkeeping, and being in charge of special projects. That was it. But something about the place felt eerie. My suspicion was even more heightened after the driver dropped my suitcases on the porch and two men rushed out of the house to collect my luggage. The men were the same height and build, and both had black hair. I would have taken them for twins, but I couldn't get a good look at their faces. Not only did they move fast, but they kept their heads down too.

"Welcome, Miss Forte," the long-legged man in the suit said, reclaiming my attention. "I am Felix, the house butler." He had an English accent.

I studied his gaunt build and stodgy disposition and then rubbed my arm as I looked over my shoulder. The driver was already behind the wheel of the car and was rolling away. Part of me wanted to run after the vehicle and beg him to take me back to the airport. I would go to every discount-travel site I knew of and shop for a cheap ticket. If my credit card payment hadn't cleared yet, I would use the money to fly back home and let my account fall into the red zone.

"Miss Forte, would you please come inside?" Felix was holding the door open and inviting me in.

What if this is a trap and, come tomorrow, I'm sold as a sex slave on the black market? I hadn't thought this whole ordeal through. Since the Christmas name was synonymous with popularity and old money, I'd never questioned whether Spencer Christmas or his proposition was completely safe. I'd felt a little too comfortable about taking the job, having spent a lot of time around people of the Christmases' caliber when attending fundraisers with my mother, who liked to show me off to donors as her proper, smart, ambitious daughter. Maybe trusting him was a mistake.

I smiled tightly at Felix, telling myself that my irrational worries were a result of anxiety—I hoped. Head up, shoulders back, I entered the house.

THE FOYER WAS WARM AND COZY, EVEN WHILE BEING spacious. The floors were light wood, and so were the walls. The space had the feeling of a luxury lodge. Everything looked new—the furniture, accessories, shelves, and artwork. Even the smell of newness sat in the air.

"When was the ranch built?" I asked the tall butler as I followed him down a wide well-lit hallway with an arched ceiling.

He kept facing forward. "I don't know, Miss Forte."

"Oh," I said, trying to think of something else to say. The fact that no one associated with Mr. Christmas wanted to carry on even the smallest conversation was concerning. "Is Mr. Christmas here today?"

"I'm not sure, Miss, Forte," the butler said, still facing forward. "However, I've been instructed to take you on a tour of the nonrestricted areas of the house."

I perked up. "There are restricted areas?"

Finally, he stopped walking and gestured toward a wide-open space to our left. "This is the dining room, where you'll have your meals. Each morning, a menu will be placed on the back of your door. You will choose your entrees for breakfast, lunch, and dinner. Snacks, along with coffee, tea, and other beverages of your choice, will be provided throughout the day. You will merely call the kitchen and ask Marta, the head chambermaid, to bring you what you like."

I opened and closed my mouth, trying to figure out what to say next. I realized he had blatantly ignored my last question. I could have pushed for an answer. But I knew it didn't matter how hard I pushed—he wasn't going to give up the house secrets and was only going to say what was permissible.

"I can make my own meals," I finally said.

"The kitchen is a restricted area. All entrances are locked." His deadpan tone matched the expression on his face.

"But what if I want a glass of water in the middle of the night?"

"Marta will see to your needs."

I gazed at him with focus. "Even at three o'clock in the morning? I wouldn't want to wake someone up so they can fetch me water at three in the morning."

Felix blinked as if waiting for my curiosity to pass. The longer the silence lingered, the more I received his message loud and clear. The rules were the rules, and he wasn't going to argue about them or allow me to change them.

I pressed my lips together in a slight grimace as he showed me the reading room, living room, sunroom, and bathrooms that I had permission to use. He showed me the staircase that went only to the third level, which was the only upper floor I was given access to. However, we didn't climb the stairs —he led me to an elevator instead.

I yawned once we were inside. The tour had reminded me how exhausted I was, and the house was so warm and so comfortably lit that all I wanted to do was shower, crawl into bed, and sleep. I restrained my second yawn after the doors slid open. The lighting in this hallway was dimmer than it was downstairs, which made me more tired. The walls were made of plaster and painted off-white. The floors were still wooden, though, and the new smell was just as pervasive as it was on the first floor.

I noticed, even though my eye sockets ached, that the hallway didn't run the length of the house. We'd just walked past the staircase and stopped in front of the only door on that level. Essentially, I was being shown to my own private wing. Felix held the door open for me, and my jaw dropped as I stepped into the space.

I sucked a quick breath. "Wow. I was not expecting this."

The room was five times larger than my last apartment. A set of stairs led down to a tastefully designed living area, featuring a burnt-orange sofa, a love seat, and two comfortable-looking armchairs that were set before floor-to-ceiling bay windows running the length of the floor and then curving around the corner. Warm light beamed from contemporary arched floor lamps. The edges of the coffee table glowed too. Beyond the windows was a wraparound patio, which held comfy lounge furniture. I'd been so enamored with the lower level that I hadn't paid attention to the largest bed I'd ever seen, to my right, and the long hallway to my left.

"The bathroom, closet, and dressing rooms are to your left, and your belongings have been put away for you." Felix picked up a remote control, pressed a button, and set it back on the white lacquered nightstand.

As a large-screen television was lowered from a pocket in the ceiling, I rubbed my temples, still processing the last part of what Felix had said. I registered him saying the dinner menu was on the bed and instructing me to make my selections and place the card on the basket attached to the back of the door. I ripped my gaze off his face, trying to remember whether or not I had packed anything that I didn't want touched. Then it appeared as if in a vision—pink plastic with two little bunny ears and only used for moments when I craved pure pleasure. My vibrator. I'd brought it.

"In the meantime, there are refreshments below. Breakfast will be served at eight, and I'll meet you in the dining room tomorrow morning at nine a.m. to escort you to the office—"

I reached out and touched him on the arm to silence him. "I'm sorry, Felix, but who put away my things? The two men who brought my luggage inside?" My face felt hot, and I was positive my skin had turned red.

With his eyebrows raised, he looked at my hand on his arm. His expression asked me to remove it, so I did. Then he carefully placed his arms by his sides and out of reach. "No, Miss Forte. The chambermaids put your belongings away."

There was no way I was going to ask if they were female, but I assumed they were. I tried to figure out where another woman might possibly put another woman's vibrator.

"Could they not do that again?" I asked, fanning myself.

"And why might that be, Miss Forte?"

"Could you stop calling me Miss Forte as well? I'm not my mother. Call me Jada." *Shit.* I hadn't meant to take that tone with him. However, I was so agitated by all the things that were bothering me at that moment.

He straightened his posture. "I can refer to you as Miss Jada if you prefer."

My lips parted rapidly as I tried to figure out what to say. *Miss Jada? Is he fucking for real?* But then I remembered that my mind had gotten ahead of me, and I had something more important to get straight. "And still"—I tried to keep the frustration out of my voice—"I don't want the chambermaids putting my things away, please." I took in a deep, steadying breath. I was exhausted beyond reasonable limits and was sure it was affecting my mood. "Sorry," I whispered.

"No apology necessary, Miss Jada."

I shook my head. "If I have to be referred to as *Ms. Someone*, then I'd rather it be *Ms. Forte*."

"Then, will that be all, Miss Forte?"

I sighed forcefully. "You never answered."

"And what have I not answered, Miss Forte?"

"I don't want chambermaids putting my things in drawers. I can do that myself. I have private shit." I closed my eyes to steady myself. "I mean private things." I opened my eyes, and he was watching me with the same blank expression.

"I will relay your request to the chambermaids," he said.

I released all the tension from my body. "Thank you."

"You're welcome, Miss Forte." He then

explained that there was a telephone on the second nightstand with directories to all the services I would need during my stay.

My eyeballs burned with tiredness when I thanked him.

He bowed his head. "Have a good evening."

I was so happy he hadn't called me Miss Forte again. As soon as I was alone, I tugged off my stinky sweater, removed my high-tops, then stamped out of my skinny jeans. The air caressing my skin had never felt so good, causing me to fall facedown on the bed.

"Umm…" I moaned as if consuming the most delicious dessert.

The soft white duvet felt divine against my skin. I closed my eyes to relish the feeling, and I kept getting more tired by the second. Before I knew it, I had given in to the need for sleep.

CHAPTER THREE

JADA FORTE

I awoke with a gasp. My eyes roamed the sleeping area before looking out at the tall windows. Black shades covered the glass. I didn't remember drawing them. Not only that, but I could have sworn I wasn't alone.

I scooted off the bed and fished my phone out of my purse. It was after three o'clock in the morning, and I'd missed two phone calls from Hope. She'd also left me a text message: *Let me know you're okay before I wake up, or I'm placing a call to local law enforcement.*

I knew she wasn't making an idle threat, so I quickly replied: *I'm fine. Fell asleep. My room is stunning. Let's talk later.*

Once I sent the message, I dropped the phone on top of the bed and rubbed my temples.

Holy shit. I'd been out like a lamp. I had never in my life slept so comfortably. The bed felt as if it had dropped from heaven. Then I remembered Felix telling me the chambermaids had packed away my luggage. Not only that, but I still hadn't showered in three—now four—days. Still groggy, I shot up from my sitting position on the side of the bed to get clean.

The bathroom was fit for any five-star hotel in the world, and the shower was large enough for an entire basketball team. I stripped off my underwear, figured out how to use the technically advanced settings to achieve my desired heat and water pressure, and then basked in the delicious droplets of water spraying from the rainfall showerhead. Washing my hair, I grinned from ear to ear, thinking I'd never before been so lucky as to land a job that came complete with a bedroom that would cost the same as a five-million-dollar apartment in Manhattan.

Yes, but you're only an assistant, I heard my mom's critical voice say in my mind.

I shook my head to banish her then finished washing my hair and used the P245 Hot Bird blow-dryer, one of the best on the market, to dry my tresses. Once my skin was no longer wet, I wrapped myself in one of the three fluffy white ankle-length robes that were in the walk-in closet, which was larger than my bedroom in my last apartment. I pulled open the drawers of the mid-century dresser that stretched the length of the wall, seeing all of my underwear and T-shirts neatly folded in two drawers at the far end of the massive piece of expensive furniture. I found my special toy in the bottom drawer.

Anyone who owned such a dresser should have a closet full of designer clothes. I liked nice clothes, but Hope and I were into shopping at vintage stores on the weekend, finding high-end designer brands for pennies on the dollar. We looked for what we called *utility garments*, such as one blouse that would go with six pairs of jeans that I already owned or a pair of pants that I could wear to work or play, night or day. Our system of shopping allowed us to do more with less, which meant my entire wardrobe couldn't come close to filling the drawers of my new room, let alone all the space for hanging clothes.

My work clothes weren't in the drawers or hanging on the bar. Then I saw a note clipped to a velvet hanger:

Dry-cleaned. Ready by 7:00 a.m. Six shirts. Six pants. Three blazers. Six blouses. Four dresses. ·

My jaw dropped. To get that many articles of clothing dry-cleaned usually would cost an arm and leg, and I'd have to wait forever to pick them up. All of this was too good to be true. I hadn't met Mr. Christmas yet and wondered if he was the embodiment of the other shoe dropping.

I didn't have to think about it just then. I almost wanted to get my toy out of the dresser, lie on my bed naked, and make myself feel even better. Instead, I remembered that I'd missed dinner, and even though Felix had given me permission to call the kitchen anytime, there was no way I was going to ask someone to prepare me a meal at four o'clock in the morning. I recalled him saying there were snacks in the living-room area. I walked downstairs and saw finger sandwiches set on a three-tiered server, silver urns labeled Coffee, Decaf, and Hot Water, and an assortment of teas, lemon slices, honey, and crushed fresh ginger. There were also fresh-baked chocolate chip, peanut butter, and oatmeal cookies and a note inviting me to ask for anything else I might like.

I devoured the sandwiches and four cookies, fixed myself a cup of mint tea with lemon, ginger, and honey, then walked to the window to stare out into the darkness. The longer I looked, the more clearly I saw an outline of the mountain range. I'd been too tired to check out the view before I fell asleep the previous day, but now I could hardly wait until the rising sun would give me a full picture of what was beyond the windows.

I WAS ABLE TO CATCH ANOTHER HOUR AND A HALF of sleep before a doorbell woke me up. I put on my robe and opened the door to two smiling ladies, who said good morning as they brought in my dry-cleaning and hung my delivery in the closet.

"Thank you so much," I said as they headed out, wanting so desperately to engage them in small talk so they could divulge all they knew about Mr. Christmas.

How excited I felt when one of them turned around and said, "Have you filled out the breakfast menu?" Her English was painted with accents of Spanish.

"No, not yet," I said.

She took the card from the back of the door and a pen out of the breast pocket on her shirt.

"You like scrambled eggs, fried eggs, eggs Benedict?" She had a very authoritative tone for such a small lady.

I stood a hair taller. "Eggs Benedict."

She checked something on the card. "Hash browns, home fries, potato au gratin?"

"Home fries."

"Bacon, turkey bacon, sausage?"

"All of it," I said.

For the first time, she looked up at me with a smile. "Pancakes?"

"Yep, those too."

"Orange juice, coffee, and tea?"

"Just coffee and mint tea."

She wrote on the menu. "And for lunch, would you like lobster roll with lobster bisque or…?"

"Say nothing more. I like that."

We smiled at each other again.

"That is good," she said. "What about dinner?"

"Surprise me."

She cocked her head. "Sorry, but you have to choose."

I pressed my lips together. Choosing from a menu every day was so unnecessary. I'd grown up in a house where I ate what was on the table, no matter what. "How about I eat whatever Mr. Christmas eats? He is here, right?"

She looked back into the hallway, where the other woman was standing, and then at me again. "I don't know."

I wanted to throw up my hands and ask them what was up with all the secrecy. Instead, I maintained decorum and smiled. "Well, if it's possible, then that's how I want it. And by the way"—I held out my hand for her to shake—"I never got your name. I'm Jada."

"Yes, Miss Forte, I'm Marta"—she pointed to the lady in the hallway—"and she is Teresa."

It took every ounce of willpower to beg her to please not call me Miss Forte. As far as I was concerned, we were all employees. All the formality wasn't necessary and was way too classist for my blood. However, it suddenly dawned on me that they all were receiving instructions from on high. I would have to ask Mr. Christmas to have them all call me by my first name.

I decided to make that one request of Mr. Christmas once we finally met face-to-face. The suspense was killing me as I hurried into the bathroom to dress for my first day of work, though I still couldn't stop yawning. I'd fallen asleep sometime between six and seven o'clock the previous day and woken up after three in the morning, which gave me roughly eight to nine solid hours of sleep. When all was said and done, I could have used ten more.

Regardless, curiosity was my fuel for the morning. I made it to the dining room, and servers entered with breakfast as soon as my butt hit the chair. The large room had a beautiful view of a crisp lake next to a grassy hill and a different part of the mountain range than the view from my room allowed.

I sighed heavily before digging in. I had never gone this long without sitting across from one of my friends to share a drink or a meal, and so soon into my new journey, I was already beginning to feel lonely.

I WAS DONE EATING BEFORE NINE AND TEXTED HOPE to let her know I was going into the office and that we should talk at six o'clock my time and nine o'clock her time. As soon as I hit Send, Felix walked into the dining room, making me jump, and asked if I was ready to go to the office.

I hopped to my feet and slid my phone into the side pocket of my blazer. "Um, sure."

Finally, I would meet the boss and learn what sort of situation I was really in. I shouldn't have listened to Hope about staying away from the Christmas family biography, but then again, I'd only had three days to get my affairs in order, so really, there hadn't been time to read it.

I followed Felix up a path of twisting and turning hallways that led to a spiraling set of stairs, and we walked down to the office. "I'm starting to think this place is a carnival fun house," I said with a chuckle.

Felix kept a straight face as his hand directed my attention. "Your desk is here."

I sighed, accepting that my last joke had bombed and letting my curious gaze roll around the room. There were two large L-shaped wooden desks with identical high-backed leather office chairs. A laptop sat on top of the one Felix directed me to. A wall of floating shelves held a printer-copier duo and other office essentials like paper, pens, pencils, and staplers.

Despite a fire kindling in the hearth, the atmosphere felt dank. I looked up at the recessed lighting, and then my glare lapped the room again.

At the end of my assessment, I jerked my neck. "Wait. There are no windows?"

"No, there aren't, Miss Forte." Felix then explained how Mr. Christmas had left detailed instructions for me, which included how to log onto the computer. "Marta will carry down a fresh pot of coffee and an assortment of teas and fixings and pastries. Unless there's something else you prefer." He looked at me in a way that said both of his ears were open and ready to receive every word that came out of my mouth.

He'd already made it clear that he wasn't willing to address my gripe about there being no windows.

I blew a hard breath out of my nostrils. "I don't need snacks. If I want them"—I patted the phone at the top right side of my desk—"I'll call the kitchen. Thank you."

"Very well. Lunch will be served at noon."

I frowned at the other empty desk, which I assumed belonged to my boss. "So this is it?"

"I'm sorry. I don't understand what you're asking for."

"I'm getting paid to follow what's on the list?"

He watched me with his favorite blank expression.

I shook my head in frustration. "Forget it. Thanks again, Mr. Felix."

His eyebrows furrowed before he bowed graciously and left me alone. I knew I'd shaken him up with that. *If he has to call me Miss Forte, then I get to show him the same sort of respect that seems to be required around here.*

I stood in silence for a while, trying to get a better grasp on my dilemma with Mr. Christmas. Despite all the space in that gigantic house, his office was in the basement. That was strange and uncomfortable and made me feel as if I was working in a tomb. But I wasn't the sort to pout for longer than a few minutes. That attitude had never worked in my mother's household. I reminded myself how much the job was paying. I had a windowless room with a soft fire brewing and nothing to complain about.

I sat at my assigned desk, opened my laptop, and started reading the list, which to my surprise was handwritten.

1. *All correspondence to those outside the office—voice, written, and video—is only to occur on this computer.*
2. *Report to the office at 9:00 a.m.*

3. *Open my email and tag each one Action Item or Informational. Write a brief summary of each.*

4. *Attend all meetings that require my presence in my stead. Take meticulous notes. Read the room. Essentially, you are me. If you receive pushback, handle it.*

5. *Place the report in the inbox near the printer. If I have a task for you to complete, you'll find it in the outbox.*

6. *Check outbox every morning to address special projects as they arise.*

7. *Finally, tend to my needs as I see fit.*

I sat up straight, rubbed the inside corners of my eyes, and read his list again. *Yes, that's exactly what he wrote.*

"Holy shit," I muttered, reading it for a third time. No wonder I was getting paid a CEO's salary. I was getting paid to be a CEO. *Not only that, but what the hell does he mean by "tend to my needs as I see fit"?*

I rubbed my forehead, wondering if that was his discreet way of saying that he was writing sex into the work plan. Mentally taxed by what I'd just read, I fell back into my seat. It still felt as if what was happening to me wasn't actually occurring. At any minute, I would wake up and see that I'd reached the end of a wild dream in which I boarded a flight to Wyoming, got stuck in an airport, and eventually ended up in this big house on a ranch, reading the weirdest list of job duties I'd ever been assigned. I couldn't picture myself appearing in important meetings as a stand-in for Mr. Spencer Christmas.

I mean, is this a joke? I imagined that Hope and my other friends were going to rush into the room and say, "Surprise! Got you!" before they all laughed their asses off and partied like it was the turn of a new century.

I shook my head, accepting that this was real life and I had a job to do to the best of my ability. I took the first step in the right direction by powering up the MacBook Pro.

I'D NEVER SEEN ANYTHING LIKE MR. CHRISTMAS'S email. There were eleven thousand unopened messages. My new boss hadn't opened a single email in seven and a half months. His email inbox was so full that it had been rejecting new messages for weeks. To get through them, I had to come up with a system to purge as many as possible without getting rid of the important ones. Sorting them all by sender helped. Most individuals sent multiple emails about the same topic. Basically, they wanted to get in touch with Mr. Christmas so that he could approve costs and new systems of operations that his corporate officers came up with. The job description said that I would be working for a finance company. I hadn't realized that he owned TFC Global. My parents had a lot of their investments parked there. The databases and files Mr. Christmas had on my computer gave me access to everything. I could even see what employees were doing on their computers in real time. And if they were away from their computers, I could still access their machines. I was pretty sure there were some privacy issues being infringed upon. I was tempted to look at my parents' investment portfolio simply because I could, but the fact that it was wrong quashed my curiosity.

"Good afternoon, Miss Forte. You're not eating lunch?"

I jumped, startled, and turned to see Marta standing at the bottom of the stairs. I rubbed my tired eyes. I'd been working for some time, and my brain felt like it was on autopilot. I caught a glimpse of the time at the top right side of my computer. It was after three.

"Damn it," I said under my breath because I was indeed starving. When I became wrapped up in work, I often forsook food until the task was complete. In the case of answering and organizing Mr. Christmas's emails—and, in effect, his life—it would have taken me forever if my system of arranging them hadn't worked. "Um, sorry I missed it."

"Do you want to eat? We'll bring it."

I told her yes, and the two men who'd brought my luggage in the previous day came down the stairs with silver-tray lunch service. As they set up on the empty side of my desk, I thanked them and Marta with a smile, and she told me to call when I was ready to have dishes cleared. They all disappeared back upstairs just about as fast as they'd appeared.

I ate the lobster roll and drank mint tea as I continued working. The number of emails in the inbox declined steadily. Soon, I'd gotten the hang of things, figuring out the demands of Mr. Christmas's business. A lot of transactions had ground to a halt because he hadn't signed off on them. I also ascertained that he'd gone missing around the time I got fired from my old job, which was a strange coincidence. There was a lot of email from his sister,

Bronwyn Henrietta Christmas, whose cursive signature was elegant, unlike the tone she took in most of her messages. My favorite from her was *You'd better tell me where you are, or I'll fart on your face.* That was quickly followed up by *Sorry Spence. That was my attempt at humor, ha, ha, ha. Why can't I track your server?* That had been in February. She reported that she was back in rehab in May. In August, she said she wanted to get the family together for the holidays, and this time, the fancy signature was replaced with a simple *Love, Bryn.*

She sent more emails asking him to please respond and whether he'd heard from Asher. I figured out he was her twin brother because she said she would be able to track him down if all that "twin telepathy bullshit" was true. The poor thing had no idea that Spencer never read any of her emails. I made sure to print out every one of them and arrange them according to date so that he could view them all.

There were some meetings taking place the next day that I was sure he would have wanted to be part of had he been more attentive when it came to his business. If I were CEO of his company, I would want to be there. A hedge-fund manager wanted to make deposits for a group of clients in foreign growth investments but needed Spencer's approval before completing the transactions. I had followed the string of emails and was up to date with that issue. The hedge-fund manager, Dillon Gross, had figured out workarounds on how to bring the project as far as he could without Spencer's full approval. I thought that was interesting and sort of wrong, as if this guy was forcing the project because he was desperate for the payoff. Most likely, I was totally wrong, of course, which was why I kept my subjective opinion out of the write-up and stuck to the facts.

"Miss Forte," Marta's voice sang. "Dinner."

She appeared at the bottom of the stairs. It was going on nine o'clock. Once again, I had lost track of time.

"Wow, Miss Marta," I said, rubbing the inside corners of my eyes. "I couldn't tell it was so late."

She touched her chest. "You called me Miss Marta?"

I felt my eyes soften along with my heart. "I figure you call me Miss Forte out of respect. And I respect you, too, so I want to do the same."

"Oh!" She sounded delighted. "No need to do that."

I cupped my hands around my mouth and whispered, "Then no need for you to call me Miss Jada."

She swiftly checked over her shoulder and then leaned toward me. "Okay. When no one is here, I call you Jada. Is that a deal?"

I extended my smile wider, even though I wanted to strangle my new boss for creating such a formal culture between employees. Employers who were that draconian usually had something to hide. Suddenly, I was struck by a realization—he did have something to hide. *But what?* I didn't know and couldn't even guess.

"That's a deal," I finally whispered.

"Now, you come to dinner. You eat. You are skinny."

I tossed my head back and laughed. Marta reminded me of my maternal grandmother—her shiny jet-black hair wrapped in a bun, her straight forehead, and her gorgeous almond eyes, high cheekbones, and bow-tie smile.

I fought the urge to slip in a question about our boss now that I had gotten her to break ranks. However, I didn't want to come off as disingenuous. I cherished the connection we were making. The short time I'd spent in the house had been extremely lonely until now. But as Marta left the room and I placed my notes in the inbox, shut down my computer, and went upstairs to the dining room, the isolation gripped me once again.

I FELT RIDICULOUS SITTING ALONE AT THE TABLE AND vowed never to do it again. From that point on, I would have my meals in either my room or my office. As I stared at the darkness beyond the window, I could hardly believe I had missed the day. It would have been nice to bundle up and go for a walk in nature at some point. I usually ran on the treadmill at the gym at least three times a week, sometimes four. I needed exercise just as much as I needed people.

If I were at home, I wouldn't have been sitting at any table, especially one like this. It was Thursday night, which meant I'd be out with Hope, Rita, Ling, Portia, and a tag-along male friend named Johnny. We'd be at Red Tar, drinking five-dollar margaritas—in New York City, that was almost like getting them for free. We went there every week, and the night always went the same way. Hope would flirt with as many cute guys as possible. I would watch, amused by her aggressive and successful style. All night, Johnny would stare at Ling—who kept up with Hope in the flirting department—because he had a massive crush on her.

Rita and Portia would spend most of the night picking out the minutest problem with each guy they saw. For instance, one guy would be bald before he was thirty-five. The other would have a potbelly before he turned forty. That guy had cruel eyes. He was stupid, he had no style, he might be a serial killer… the criticisms went on and on and on until Rita and Portia each found that one guy who didn't have any flaws worth discussing. Once they'd each beamed on Mr. Right for Tonight, I wouldn't see them until the next time we decided to go out.

I would usually run into groups of people I'd met on the many previous Thursdays when we'd graced the scene at Red Tar and had a ball chatting about the conversation topics of the night, which could include how someone had found a rat in her oven and six exterminators told her to just cook it.

"The barbarians!" I would reply.

One person might say he saw Taylor Swift singing "I Knew You Were Trouble" in the subway station the week before. Someone else would confirm that it wasn't her, but someone else would say it absolutely was. A song everyone loved would play, and we'd all start singing, dancing, and drinking until four in the morning, when the bar shut down and everyone stumbled out onto the sidewalk in all phases of intoxication.

I took a moment to relive one of the best Thursday nights at Red Tar I'd ever experienced. I saw myself fawning over a Chris Hemsworth look-alike and boldly introducing myself. Hope always said my problem was I was attracted to the guys all the other girls in the world were attracted to as well. Usually, a guy like that would have about fifty hyenas around him, snapping at him, ready to strip off their clothes and be fucked by him. But that night, I got to the Adonis first simply because I was the one he wanted. He flashed me a big white toothy grin and enthusiastically extended his hand for me to shake. His gaze embraced me as if I were the most beautiful woman in the world. He asked what I did for a living, and I said I was in PR. He was a hedge-fund manager but loved the idea of saving enough money to retire to a farm in Vermont and live there for the rest of his life with a woman who had my kind of tits.

"Good evening, Miss Forte," a man said.

My eyes popped open. I hadn't realized I'd

closed them. *Shit.* Not only had I been fantasizing, but I also hadn't realized how exhausted I was, which was strange. Ever since I'd become a full-fledged New Yorker, sleep didn't tell me when to go to bed—I told sleep when *I* was ready to go to bed. Apparently, that had changed.

"Good evening," I said, mustering a smile.

I didn't know the server's name, but he placed a covered plate in front of me and lifted the top. The food looked delectable, and the smell that rose to my nostrils was divine.

The guy took a step back, matching my smile. "You have cracked pepper filet mignon and butter, onion and garlic roasted new potatoes with orange-glazed baby carrots. And would you like white or red wine?"

There was no use asking him his name, even though I'd won a small hard-fought victory in getting Marta to open up. It dawned on me that there was a reason why I was so insistent on learning everyone's names—the solitude was consistently getting to me.

I felt a thickness in my throat as I forced myself to not cry. "Red," I chirped, pointing at the bottle of wine sitting on the silver serving cart.

With one hand behind his back, the server stood

with perfect posture and poured the red liquid into a stemmed glass. When he left, my shoulders slumped as fatigue grabbed hold of me. I felt the only thing that could energize me was to run upstairs to my palace of a bedroom, pack my things, and get the hell out of that house. But I had no money and would have to call my mother for help.

I resolved to bite the bullet and was doing just that when my cellphone chimed. I took the device out of my pocket. Once I saw the name on the screen, the tears I'd been holding back rushed into my eyes.

"Hope," I said, wiping the tears from my cheeks.

"Jada? Are you crying?"

I sniffed. "A little."

"But why?" she asked in a soft and sympathetic tone.

My gaze rolled around the enormous dining room and stopped at the darkness beyond the window. I sighed. "I haven't even met my boss."

Hope gasped. "You mean you haven't met Spencer Christmas yet?"

"No."

"That's odd."

"I know," I said with a sigh. "But my room… oh my God, Hope. I have to send you pics. It's five times bigger than my apartment and feels like a luxury suite at a five-star hotel."

"That sounds fun."

"Yeah…" I cradled the phone closer to my ear. "But still… I want to go home," I whispered as if someone could hear me. But there was no one around. I was totally alone.

Hope remained silent. "Listen, Jada," she finally said. "You know I love the idea of you coming back to the city. Last night, I went to Red Tar with Rita and Portia, and with all the fucking criticizing, they nearly gave me a brain injury. But are you really ready to give up forty thousand a month?"

I sighed heavily as I slumped in my seat. "I don't know. Yes. No. Maybe. It's not like I have the money to get the hell out of here in the first place. I'm flat broke."

"Hello. I'm Spencer Christmas."

I sat up quickly and turned to see who had said that. My jaw dropped. Standing not that far from me was the man from all the pictures of Spencer Christmas I had studied—tall and graceful and in real life even more stunningly handsome.

CHAPTER FOUR

JADA FORTE

"Jada?" Hope asked, sounding worried. "Are you still there?"

I kept my expanded eyes on my new boss. "Hope, I have to go."

"Wait? Is it him?" she asked, sounding super curious.

I cleared my tight throat. "Um, yes," I said in as professional a way as I could, though my voice was hoarse.

"Fucking shit!" she exclaimed. "Is he hot?"

"Good night, Hope." *Hell yes—totally hot.* "We'll talk soon. Love you." I wanted to hang up right away, but it was common courtesy to wait until she said it back.

"Love you too. And, Jada, call me and tell me

all about your first encounter with the phantom of the ranch."

"Will do," I said and finally hung up.

I scooted my chair back, but before I could stand, he threw up a hand. "Stay seated."

I slowly lowered my bottom back to the chair. "Good evening, Mr. Christmas. I didn't know you were joining me." My skin tingled all over, and a heavy feeling settled into my stomach. Suddenly, I was so hungry I could eat a horse. I could not look away or banish the surprise from my expression as he took a seat at the head of the table.

He nodded toward my plate. "Would you like something else to eat?"

My shocked gaze fell on my dinner. I could hardly discern what I was looking at. "Um, no, I'm fine."

"Then you should eat," he said, pointing with an open hand as if inviting me to do so.

I didn't want to do anything but study him some more. There was something telling about his face. The skin beneath his eyes was swollen. His eyes were red, and the lids appeared to be so heavy that he could hardly keep them open.

Finally, I picked up my knife and fork, and more because I was hungry than to appease him, I began to cut into the tender steak. I felt as if I had to say something or else he might disappear into thin air. "So, Mr. Christmas. I'm happy you could join me. It was getting lonely around here." I smiled from ear to ear.

His frown intensified as I brought a bite of meat to my lips. I felt he was waiting for me to put it in my mouth, so I did.

"Your mother is Patricia Forte, isn't she?" he asked while I was chewing.

"Uh-hum," I said, irritated that he would bring her up so fast. That could mean one of two things. The first possibility was that she was the one who'd gotten me the job, which meant she wanted something from him and he wanted something from her. The second was that he'd hired me simply because Patricia Forte was my mother and he wanted something from her and planned to have me mediate.

I swallowed quickly then dropped my utensils and folded my arms on my chest. "Why are you asking about my mother?"

He frowned at my knife and fork as if unhappy that I had let go of them. Then his glare found my face again. "You don't like talking about your mother?"

I felt my eyebrows squeezing together. "It depends."

Silence fell between us, but I couldn't ignore the fact that we were staring at each other. He was certainly picking me apart. His eyes freely roamed my face and then ventured down the front of my neck. I could tell that he purposely stopped them from dropping farther by the forceful way in which his eyes rose back to my face.

He skimmed his jawline with his fingers. "On what?"

I tried not to be hypnotized by the way he was watching me. "Is she the reason you hired me?" If she was, I would be obligated to quit.

"Yes and no," he said.

I stared intently, waiting for an explanation.

"Mostly, it was your résumé that made me extend an offer of employment to you," he said. "However, your mother's been in the public eye since you were very young. It was the same for me." His right eye narrowed shrewdly. "I've seen photos of you at fundraisers with Patricia Forte. Your mother is a powerful politician. She didn't get that way by not using all of her assets, and you are certainly one of them."

I shook my head decisively. "I'm nothing like my mother."

He paused to examine me then folded his arms. "What do you think your mother's like?"

My mouth was caught open. The answer I had was long and whiny and surely not for him to hear. I would never tell him, or anyone besides Hope, that I thought my mother was narcissistic, which was why I didn't share much of what was going on in my life with her. My mother still had no idea that I'd been let go from my last job. She would have taken my layoff personally and moved mountains to secure me another position, only it would be a position with one of her friends, donors, or colleagues—one that ultimately benefitted her in one way or another. I couldn't tell Spencer Christmas that I usually avoided her phone calls and responded to her voice messages with texts that had lots of smiley faces and declarations of how great everything was going even if my life was in the shitter. It was already early December—she would expect me home for the Christmas holiday as she did each year. The thought of gracing her doorstep and sleeping in my old room, where she could easily have access to me, made my stomach queasy.

"You see?" Spencer Christmas said.

I blinked to bring his face back into focus. "What do I see?"

His probing gaze made me chew nervously on my lower lip. *What the hell is he looking for?*

Then he shifted abruptly in his seat. "By the way, how do you like your room?"

I felt my whole body sigh in relief as I welcomed the change in subject. "I like it very much." *I wish he would stop looking at me that way.*

"I see. If you prefer a different room, I can have one arranged for you. I thought you might like the view of the lake." He paused, but his eyes continued to penetrate me. "I heard you say you wanted to go home."

I squeezed my eyes shut as I sighed. "Ahh... you heard that?"

"I want you to be comfortable while you're here."

I turned my head slightly. "Is that so?"

He eyed me suspiciously. "I wouldn't have said it if I hadn't meant it."

"Then why is everyone hell-bent on referring to me as Miss Forte? That doesn't make me feel comfortable."

Spencer Christmas pressed his back against the chair. "When you say *everyone*, who exactly do you mean?"

"Felix, for one."

"He's a butler. He'll only refer to you in the formal way. Who else?"

"Marta and Theresa seemed as if they were afraid to tell me their names. What's that about?"

For the first time since arriving, Spencer Christmas showed me his rendition of a smile, which was actually a smirk—and a sexy, mouthwatering one at that. But the expression faded just as fast as it had made its brief appearance.

"You left someone behind in New York. Is that why you want to go home?" He enfolded his fingers on top of the table. "Because I skimmed the notes you made today. They're exactly what I was looking for. So you can do the job."

I turned my head. "Are you fucking with me?" My eyes grew wide. I hadn't meant to curse.

His smirk made another appearance. "I asked you a simple question?"

"And I asked you one too."

He nodded thoughtfully. "You don't like being referred to as Miss?"

"No." I pressed my lips into a hard line.

"And what do you prefer?"

"Jada. Just Jada. But why all the secrecy in the first place?"

Spencer Christmas leaned away from me and grimaced. "My staff is professional, Jada. They're from some of the most famous households in the country, and their salaries reflect that. They understand they're being paid to exercise a healthy amount of discretion, especially with houseguests."

"But I'm not a guest. I'm an employee."

"If you do not reside in the residence permanently, then you are a guest who is working for me under contract."

I folded my arms. "I haven't signed a contract."

"Yes, you have."

"When?"

"When you accepted the terms of your six month assignment."

I nodded thoughtfully. "Ah, I see. That's fair." I smiled to show him that I agreed with him and our back-and-forth about the behavior of his employees had been resolved with my acceptance of his explanation.

His lips built into a slow but slight smile as his eyes smoldered. My nerves tingled, which surprised the hell out of me. I wasn't the sort of girl who got this flustered by every good-looking Adonis of a man.

"And now, Jada…" His voice was so sexy. "I want an answer to my question."

If only I had conveniently forgotten what he'd asked. But I remembered. It was stuck in the forefront of my mind, but I hadn't been able to come up with an answer.

I stopped bouncing my knee. "Are you asking if I left behind a boyfriend in New York?"

I held my breath as he gave a gentle nod.

I chewed on my lower lip as the word *virgin* lit up in my mind like the marquee above Times Square. My skin warmed as the truth wanted to gush out of my mouth like a confession.

And again, he gave me a look I couldn't interpret. I cleared my throat. "Um, only friends. No boyfriends."

I could feel him watching me intently as I cut a piece of steak and popped it into my mouth, operating under the assumption that as long as I was chewing, I didn't have to speak. Finally, Spencer Christmas grunted intriguingly. Just the sound sent a warm sensation through my thighs. Never had such robust sexual responses gone off inside me.

"But you're very beautiful," he said almost as if it were an afterthought.

Keep your composure, Jada, I kept repeating to myself. His tone and the way he looked away when he softly spoke those words made me feel as if I was the most beautiful girl in the world. The fact that I wanted to leap out of my seat, jump on his lap, and beg him to be my first also shocked me. I had guarded my virginity like a pit bull, perhaps because it was the only thing of mine that Patricia hadn't tried to blatantly control. I figured she never liked to picture me having sex, so she stayed away from the topic.

He stood abruptly. "Enjoy your meal." His curt tone matched his frown.

I blinked rapidly, shocked that he was leaving. For some reason, I felt we should be together every single moment as long as I was in the house. It was crazy, of course, but I couldn't help feeling that way. I also noticed he was wearing camouflage cargo pants. They were over washed and dusty looking, so different from the clean black T-shirt he wore. The pants threw me off. He seemed so cultivated, the sort of guy who wore Armani or Brioni and never got dirty and certainly didn't wear the sort of clothing men wore to do manual labor.

All I could do was nod.

He made for the exit and then turned back to face me. "By the way, have you read the book?"

My thoughts froze. "What book?"

His eyes narrowed. "The biography about my family."

"Oh…" Now I remembered. "No. I haven't."

"I prefer that you don't," he said and continued out of the room.

I pressed my hand over my heart, feeling it race. Then I looked down at my crotch. *Holy shit.* I was certain my panties were soaking wet. A giddy energy raced through me as my curiosity about Spencer Christmas burned like a forest fire. I had to know more about him. He hadn't said not to read the book. He'd said he *preferred* that I not read it. There was a difference. I certainly had to read it now. I vowed to order the e-book version before going to bed.

CHAPTER FIVE

JADA FORTE

My alarm blared, and I groaned as I pressed the most comfortable pillow I'd ever slept on over my face. I'd set it for seven-thirty after taking a shower and sliding into bed the night before. Once I got myself settled between the soft sheets, I was too tired to order the book *The Dark Christmases*. Also, it cost $14.99, and my bank account was overdrawn by $263.76 because an automatic payment to a credit card I hadn't accounted for had gone through. I felt so inadequate. I was pretty sure Spencer Christmas would rather bang and date women who could afford a $14.99 book. I'd decided the best thing I could do was go right to sleep, knowing that one day soon, I'd be able to pay off that credit card and all the others.

I reached over to the nightstand, grabbed my phone, and turned off the alarm. Then I forced myself to sit on the edge of the bed to gather my bearings. An overwhelming feeling of being a loser swept over me as I remembered the red numbers showing negative $263.76.

"Maybe I should ask Mr. Christmas for an advance," I said, rubbing my eyes. Then I recalled every bit of our conversation from the previous night. "No." I sighed then jumped up and headed to the closet to get dressed. I would not ask him for an advance or request that he be my first sexual partner, even though I wanted both.

I PUT ON A PENCIL SKIRT AND A TIGHT V-NECK sweater. I felt so shameless, hoping he would come down to the office that day and notice the boobs I was showing off. I stared at myself in the standing mirror in the dressing room.

"What the hell are you doing, Jada Forte?" I whispered. *Get a grip.* I had to get my hands on that fucking book.

I quickly checked the time on my wristwatch and then switched my pencil skirt for a more sensible pair of black slacks. I debated whether to change my sweater but decided to keep it on. Then I rushed back into the bedroom to use up some of my extra minutes to call Hope for advice on how to handle my new boss, should he decide to join me in the office. She answered on the first ring, as she did whenever she was available.

"I've been waiting for you darling! What happened last night? Did you fuck him?" she said excitedly.

I rolled my eyes as my buttocks clamped down on the foot of the bed. "Are you really asking me that?"

She paused. "You're right. I would've fucked him, not you. But nevertheless, what happened between the two of you?"

I chuckled as my heart soared, remembering the dopamine hits I got just from being near him. "Not much. I ate dinner, and he asked me questions."

"Wait, he didn't eat with you?" she said, although I wasn't sure why that mattered.

"No," I said, hoping she'd explain.

"That's strange."

"Is that your complete take on the situation—it

was strange—or do you detect that he chose not to eat for another reason? And is that reason written in the book *The Dark Christmases*?" I said it so fast that I had to take a breath.

"Wow, Jada, you're really hopped up on adrenaline. I've never heard you this way before."

I shot to my feet. "What? Yes, you have."

But she was right. I'd never felt this out of control in my life, not even when I was down to my last couple of dollars. Not even while I was stuck in the airport, smelling not so good and desperately trying to figure out how to get myself on the first flight to Jackson Hole.

"You're into him. I told you he was your type, didn't I?"

Did she? I shook my head adamantly. "He's not my type." But I hated being dishonest with myself or to Hope. "Okay, he's my type," I whispered. "Shit, Hope, I can't stop thinking about him. That's why I need that book. I need to know why I should stay away, despite his looks and his general verve…"

"Verve? Did you just say 'verve'?" she asked, sounding shocked.

"Mm-hmm," I said cautiously. "Why the reaction to 'verve'?"

"Listen… and I'll make this short because I'm

cutting into my beauty sleep. You do know how early it is here, and I didn't get to bed until three."

I raised my eyebrows as I nodded, remembering how that felt. It was easy to lose track of time in the city. So many times, I'd shown up at my desk and run that day's PR event fueled on four hours of sleep and four cups of coffee.

"Ah," I said, dropping my head back to rub my temples. "Shit, I forgot about the time difference. Do you want me to call you back later?"

"Yes," she said decisively. "I want you to call me a lot, and I'll call you, too, but for now, I have something very important that you should hear."

I frowned, disturbed, as I automatically sat back down on the bed. "What?"

"Do not fuck Spencer Christmas. You've never owned up to it, but I know you're a virgin, Jada Forte. I don't recommend you read the book either. The shit that's written about him is, like, way out there. He doesn't have the sort of unsullied dick that should fall into your virginal pussy. But I know he is like finding ice water after being stranded for days in a hot desert. So… if you decide to ignore my warning and drink, make him wear a condom or two."

"Yikes," I said, gritting my teeth. "Then he's promiscuous?"

"That's an understatement. But he's also fucked up. You know I hate being judgmental, and you know I love a good comeback story, but make sure he's come back before you do anything with him."

My posture perked up. "Come back from what?"

She sighed hard. "Jada, you have good instincts. You know how fucking weird you said he's acting?"

"Yeah…" I couldn't remember actually articulating that he was behaving weirdly, even though he was, and heck, so was I.

"Until he stops acting that way, don't fuck him."

I wanted to question Hope until she was forced to take back what she'd said, but my friend was not the type to issue warnings lightly. I told her I would heed her words. However, the truth was that I would *try* to heed her warning. We both said we loved and missed each other and made a plan to figure out how we were going to spend New Year's Eve together. She also mentioned that we should meet me in LA after I got my first check because there was no way in the world she was going to Milwaukee.

"Wyoming," I said.

"Okay, there either."

I had a good laugh before hanging up. When I left the room, I was determined to keep it only business between Spencer Christmas and me, and I was so hungry I could eat breakfast twice. So I left my room for the day and skipped down the stairs, and as soon as I sat down at the dining room table, I was served an egg-white omelet with cheddar cheese, spinach, grilled onions, and mushrooms.

I pulled up that day's *Times* on my phone. Of course, my mother was on the political pages. There was what I called "Congress chaos," and my mom had put herself in the middle of it, stoking the flames with her sound bites. She loved the game of politics more than she loved my dad and sometimes even more than me.

"How do you like the omelet?"

I looked up quickly, my belly fluttering as I stared wide-eyed at the gorgeous face of Spencer Christmas.

"Um…" I had to close my mouth and force myself to swallow. "It's good," I whispered as I narrowly avoided choking.

He put both hands on the top of a chair and clenched it. "And how did you sleep last night?"

"Um," I said, shifting in my seat. "The bed is

very comfortable." Goodness, he made me so nervous.

His eyes smoldered as if something about me excited him. "Good." He cleared his throat.

We watched each other in awkward silence. I wanted to touch him. I wanted him to wrap me in his arms. He was wearing the same pants he'd had on the night before, but this time, he had on a long-sleeved black sweatshirt.

I ignored my curiosity and forced a pleasant smile onto my face. "Are you going to join me?"

"You did good work yesterday. Thank you," he said curtly, wearing what seemed like his perpetual frown, then left the room just as fast as he'd entered it.

I breathed heavily, feeling winded, and I made myself calm down. I couldn't read the article about my mother or about anyone else, for that matter. My mind was too cluttered with visions of Spencer Christmas.

Suddenly, my phone dinged, alerting me that I had a new deposit in my bank account. My jaw dropped when I saw the amount. "Fourteen thousand dollars," I whispered. The deposit had been made by someone named Pete Sykes and was noted as an advance on my salary plus reimbursement for the troubles I'd encountered during my journey to Jackson Hole.

When I could finally close my mouth, I swallowed the excess moisture.

"Pete Sykes," I said low enough not to be heard, hopefully. Hope had warned me to trust my instincts, and I was beginning to wonder if somehow Mr. Christmas had heard me complain to Hope about how broke I was.

But who is Pete Sykes, and why is he the one paying me? I sat up tall as my eyes shifted from left to right and then back to the left. Knowing exactly what I had to do next, I went to the online store and bought *The Dark Christmases.*

CHAPTER SIX

JADA FORTE

He had addressed the notes I'd put into the inbox the previous day and added some of his own. Spencer Christmas reminded me that he already instructed me to sit in on meetings requiring his presence. *I'm not available so just do it*, he'd written. I conjured in my mind a picture of him saying that. He'd never looked so hot, and I'd never felt so flushed.

The first person I called was Lass Olsen, the chief operating officer of TFC Global. My caller ID must have shown up as Spencer Christmas, because right away, Lass Olsen said, "Where the hell have you been?"

"Hello, Mr. Olsen," I said.

"Who's this?" he snapped.

Then I remembered what my mother said to all her aides when it came to the power game—figure out when to give expected answers and when not to give them. She would fire those who couldn't figure it out. She called it the art of power-playing.

I grunted dismissively and sat up straight. "I called to advise you that I will be sitting in on all the meetings in which Mr. Christmas's presence is wanted and required. Please have your secretary send me any dial-in or videoconferencing details."

"You didn't answer my question. Who the fuck are you?"

"I'm aware of that." I paused. There was the gracious moment of silence that I'd hoped for. My next step was to fill it before he did. "Mr. Olsen, I'm here to help you get the process running smoothly again. When I hang up, I'm going to send you and others all the answers to questions that have been building for the past ten months. And by the way, my name is Jada Forte."

He mumbled something incoherent and then said, "Okay."

I quickly concluded the call and two hours later had sent all the replies to the emails that had gone unanswered for quite some time.

I was at the start of my first videoconference

when Marta and another server brought coffee, tea, and an assortment of scones and set them on my desk so that I could easily serve myself. I smiled and winked at them before they exited, and they returned the gesture, which made me smile.

"Excuse me, Jada Forte. Do you find this topic amusing?" Lass Olsen asked. He turned out to be a balding man in his late thirties.

I kept my eyes from growing wide as all the attendees around the table scrutinized my image on the big screen in their office. These were the times when coming of age under the tutelage of my mother paid off.

"Never mind me." I made sure my tone was authoritative and even. "Continue." I watched them all as if expecting them to do just as I said.

Lass's eyebrows furrowed and then released as he went on about new business. Every now and then, I would catch someone looking at me, but I listened and jotted down what I thought was important for Mr. Christmas to know. I had another meeting with an investment banker under Mr. Christmas's employ who was pitching a major project. I hadn't expected Lass to be present during that meeting, but he was—and he sat in on the next three meetings as well. It was clear he was monitoring me. I understood his concern, of course. I was young and a face he'd never seen before, so there was no need to insist he give me some fucking breathing room.

Marta had already delivered lunch, and I had asked her to bring me dinner, too, since I would be working well into the night. This time, I asked for something simple and not messy, like a grilled cheese sandwich with a garden salad, and that was exactly what she brought me, along with a classic tiramisu for dessert.

It was going on ten o'clock at night when I was finally ready to place my thick set of notes in the inbox and head upstairs for bed. However, a chill ran down my spine, and I quickly turned toward the entrance and then the fireplace and folded my arms, waiting for that eerie feeling of being watched to pass. Perhaps Spencer Christmas was way too much on my mind. I had missed him and had been too busy to obsess about my hope that he'd come in and check on me at some point during the day. My eyes were so tired they burned, and all I could think about was stripping off my clothes and getting into bed, which was probably why my inhibitions were lowered just a bit.

I rushed over to the floating shelves, snatched a

Post-it out of the holder, and wrote, *Are you going to avoid me for most of the time that I'm here?*

I played with the piece of paper between my fingers before sticking it on top of the thick stack of papers I was leaving for Mr. Christmas.

"What the hell," I whispered on my way out.

I DIDN'T EVEN SHOWER. I STRIPPED OUT OF ALL MY clothes and climbed into the comfortable sheets, which felt like heaven against my skin. As soon as my head hit the pillow, I was out. I didn't wake up until my alarm chimed at five in the morning. My first meeting was at ten o'clock Eastern Standard Time, which meant I had to be showered, fed, and ready for work by at least six o'clock my time.

I'd missed a call from Hope, but she left a voice message: "You haven't fucked him yet, have you?"

I chuckled and responded by texting: *Not yet.*

Suddenly, I gasped and sat up straight. "Not yet" implied that I would at some point end up having sex with my new boss. That was very presumptuous of me. I wanted to take back my response, but it was too late—I'd already put it out into the universe. Plus, Hope hadn't replied yet, which could only mean that she was on her way to the office or getting ready for court. Hope was a public defender.

Suddenly, I buried my face in my palms as I remembered the note I'd left Mr. Christmas while in my intoxicated state of exhaustion. "Shit," I muttered, ruing having to step back into the office and face his reaction to my blatant flirting. *What the hell was I thinking?* I crossed my fingers and hoped to God that if I moved fast enough, I could get to the inbox and pull the Post-it off the report before he saw it.

There was no time to shower. I wiped up with a warm washcloth then brushed my teeth, washed my face, and reapplied enough makeup to look fresh and pretty just in case I ran into Spencer Christmas unexpectedly. Before leaving the room, I rang the kitchen and let the staff know I'd be having break-fast in the office and requesting that they serve me whatever Mr. Christmas was having.

"He's not eating breakfast," Marta said.

I felt a hard knot form in my heart as I paused, wondering why not.

"But you can order whatever you like, Jada," Marta said, my name rolling easily off her tongue.

I looked heavenward and thanked my lucky

stars that he more than likely wasn't on the property, which meant he probably hadn't read my note.

I ordered eggs Benedict with fresh fruit and light-roast coffee and a cup of mint green tea for later. A weight had been lifted off my shoulders as I strolled confidently to the elevator and made a pact with myself to never ever break professionalism with Mr. Christmas again, even if the last time I'd seen him, he'd looked at me a few times as if he wanted to rip my clothes off. I gazed up at the ceiling, trying to picture every time he'd done that.

The soft ding of the doors sliding open broke my fantasy of him throwing me on the table, spreading my legs, and thrusting his hard cock inside me, ending my days as a virgin. I stepped out of the elevator before the doors closed and stopped to pinch the bridge of my nose. I scolded my mind for imagining such naughtiness between my boss and me. *Bad brain.* As soon as I was able to completely banish the picture of us getting it on, I walked to the office as fast as I could, bypassing my desk and heading straight for the inbox.

I gasped. The box was empty. My heart sank.

I looked at the outbox, which had papers in it and a sticky on top that read, *Your angst is duly noted.*

My legs grew weak. I looked for something to sit

on and managed to make it to one of the club chairs in front of the unlit fireplace. I plopped my rear into it. *My angst is duly noted?*

I covered my face with my hands and said, "Shit, shit, shit," into my palms. As I was quietly swearing, I heard a sound similar to heat turning on. I removed my hands in time enough to see fire erupting in the fireplace.

My body quickened, and I scooted to the edge of the seat. It was as if it had been lit just for me. My examining eyes roamed the room as that feeling of being watched returned with a vengeance. But I saw nothing that resembled a camera. Perhaps it was in my mind. I checked my watch. I still had enough time to complete some important tasks before my first videoconference of the day. Forgetting all about that weird sensation of being watched and the strange—and, actually, promising—reply from Mr. Christmas, I doubled down on my vow to keep it strictly business between him and me, and I went to my desk and got to work.

THE DAY WAS GOING A LOT LIKE THE DAY BEFORE. I was certainly earning every dollar of my high salary. Another skill I'd adopted from my mother was devising a system that worked and sticking to it. I would take notes and ask those who wanted input from Mr. Christmas to be clear about what they needed to say to him and the outcome they were seeking. By the third meeting, Lass Olsen had sent me an email to say that I was doing a fine job of getting the ball rolling again. I knew I was winning him over because by our last meeting of the day, he stopped scowling whenever he had to say something to me.

I'd forgone lunch, but I didn't miss dinner at my desk. Once again, we decided to keep it simple. I had a juicy Angus beef burger and crispy steak fries. I rubbed the corners of my eyes after writing the last task, which Spencer Christmas was to address. Then without thinking about it, I snatched a sticky out of the holder.

I knew what was fueling me. I had gone another whole day without Spencer Christmas even making a short appearance. I missed his energy.

My hand seemed to have a mind of its own as I wrote, *People are missing you!*

One exclamation mark wasn't enough, so I added two more.

THE NEXT MORNING, I RAN STRAIGHT TO THE outbox. I pressed my hand over my frantically beating heart when I saw the yellow Post-it stuck to a piece of paper. I jerked my head back in surprise as a quarter of my attention registered that he'd only written one flimsy page in response to everything I'd put in his inbox. The Post-it on top read, *You'll see me soon.*

I shook my head repeatedly, wondering what to make of his response. My note had said *people* were missing him. It hadn't said I was missing him.

Am I that transparent? I closed my eyes and groaned. I was.

I stuck the Post-it on the back of the single page of his notes as I walked back to my desk. Then I stopped in my tracks to finish reading what he'd written. I was not supposed to turn on my computer that day. He said he'd handled my scheduled meetings, so no one would be expecting me to attend any of them. Someone named Martin would be meeting me in the foyer at noon to take me to the atrium.

"The atrium?" I whispered and looked around

to see if anyone else was reading the note. Of course, no one was.

The fire ignited in the fireplace, and I jumped, startled. I put my notes, along with Spencer's reply, in the top drawer of my desk and then sat in my chair and stared at my computer. I'd been working nonstop ever since I started the job, and frankly, I didn't know what to do with myself other than head back upstairs and sleep for another two hours. It was as if I'd gotten used to functioning while being excessively exhausted. But truth be told, I hadn't fully recovered from my arduous journey to the ranch. It was Friday, and I had the weekend off. I had no doubt I would sleep in the next day and indulge in the book about Mr. Christmas's family as well.

There was no need to defy my boss's directives, but I so badly wanted to. I couldn't hide the fact that I was pissed off at him for staying away from me. I'd never wanted to see somebody's face again as much as I did his.

Figuring I'd call the only person I could complain to, I took my cellphone out of the pocket of my cross-body bag and called Hope. That was exactly what I did, but my call went straight to voicemail. I didn't even leave a message. Instead, I pouted about how my move across the country was making it difficult to connect with the one person I loved as a sister.

I texted: *Just called you. Hate this game of phone tag. Miss you. Love you. Call me.*

I sighed as I put the phone back into the pouch. That feeling of isolation was back and stronger than ever. Then I asked to have breakfast brought to my room. There was no way I was sitting at the big lonely table by myself ever again. I had the classic American with scrambled eggs, bacon, pancakes, and hash browns. Marta told me that was what Mr. Christmas was having. Butterflies fluttered in my stomach with the thought that he was somewhere on the premises. *What does he do all day long, anyway?*

I ate in the lower level of my room, sitting on the sofa and gazing out over the wet fields of grass, trees and mountains in the distance. The landscape was made even more picturesque by the lake. I realized that before, I hadn't the opportunity to just sit and take in my beautiful natural surroundings. I put my feet up on the ottoman and grew more relaxed as I ate and tracked all the political news of the day on my phone, looking for anything written about my mother. I was quite aware that I would have rather read *The Dark Christmases*, but in a few hours,

I had a tour with this Martin guy I'd never met, and didn't want to start reading, and then have to stop so abruptly.

———

AT SOME POINT DURING MY READING, I LEARNED about how my mother was initiating some useless vote that was a ploy to score political points with her base. My mother never stopped playing the game of politics, which was why she had been a congresswoman for nearly twenty-seven years, winning her first election right before I turned two. And knowing my mother, she must have had me, her only child, in order to appeal to working mothers. That was another thing about my mother—she was shameless, which was why I always searched to see if I was registering anywhere in her actions and schemes.

When I was in college, oftentimes people would come up to me and say they didn't know I'd endorsed a certain movement or law. After researching what the hell they were talking about, I would learn that my mom had used me to say that her only daughter made her come around on an issue that she couldn't give two fucks about other than that it appealed to people in my age bracket and scored her some new votes. Of course, it was bull crap. She never asked about my political ideologies. She didn't care which party I belonged to or know that every time I stood in the voting booth, staring at the ballot, I struggled with voting for her instead of one of her opponents. I knew that if she lost, my life would change for the better.

I was glad to know my name hadn't popped up in her politics, at least for that day. That was one reason why I was able to submit to my heavy eyelids and fall asleep.

The doorbell woke me. I thought I was dreaming until I heard it again. My head groggy, I shot to my feet and checked my watch.

"Shit," I muttered. I had overslept. I was supposed to be in the foyer to meet someone named Martin twenty minutes earlier.

I rushed to answer the door as fast as I could.

CHAPTER SEVEN

SPENCER CHRISTMAS

I shifted abruptly to scratch the back of my neck. It wasn't itching, but I had to do something with the anxiety in my body. "I'm questioning my decision to hire her."

"Is her work not up to par?" Dr. Mita Sharma asked. I flew her in from Manhattan once a week for therapy.

I sat up tall as I cleared my throat. "That's not the problem. I knew she would excel at the job."

"Okay, then, why are you questioning your decision to employ her?"

I sighed forcefully and scrubbed my face with both hands. There was no way of sugarcoating it. A man who was ready to take ownership of his wrongdoings shared them and took the penalty of being judged like a man.

I looked Mita steadily in the eye. "I watch her sleep."

"Oh," she said with a rise in her vocal pitch.

I looked away from her gaze. "I can't stop watching her."

"Okay…"

"But it's more than that."

She remained silent in the way that she normally did when she was giving me a chance to explain. The woman was a good listener, which was one reason I'd gone back after our first session. She hadn't merely listened to me—she'd actually heard me. Her dark hair was shiny, and her copper skin hadn't a blemish. Her dark almond eyes were more than sensual—they were deep, peering, and able to see within my soul. I knew myself. I needed her to be my therapist. I needed to respect someone who looked like her on a different level other than wanting to fuck. And I hated fucking—always had.

I revealed this to her. I even told her about my first time, which had been with a prostitute. My father watched us. I was supposed to show him I knew how to fuck like a man. But I couldn't keep my dick up or get off. My father then pushed me off the girl, who was probably my age—thirteen—and handled her as though she were trash, fucking her as if she was a rag doll. He made me keep trying with different prostitutes until I got it right. When I finally got off with some poor girl who probably had a hard time at home before she ran away and fell into the clutches of the old letch who was my father, Randolph shook my shoulder, congratulating me on finally becoming a man. It was the first time he'd ever commended me for doing anything.

My reputation as a playboy used to make my old man proud. I dated lots of women—beautiful, famous, all the sort who thought their value came from how they looked and what was between their legs. I struggled through fucking them once or twice and then never again. They all wondered what was wrong with me. I made excuses, like I had work or was too tired to fuck. On many occasions, I would pick a fight or say something harsh to make them not want to have sex with me. When they finally had enough of my bullshit and broke up with me, I was happy. I didn't like having my dick stimulated until the first year I came home from college.

The memories made me shudder, so I quickly

replaced them with the knowledge that my dick hadn't gotten wet in years. It hadn't gotten hard either. No porn, no prostitutes, no jerking off, and no fantasizing about my therapist—or any other woman, for that matter. For the first time in a long time, I felt free roaming in my asexual universe— and then Jada arrived. I was shocked that I was so fucking attracted to her. I'd seen photos of Jada before I hired her, but she made a hell of an impact in person. I'd also investigated her thoroughly. I knew everything about her parents, her last job, and why she'd been let go. I knew about her best friend, Hope Callaway, a lawyer in Manhattan and a damn good one at that. But I couldn't find out whether or not Jada Forte had a boyfriend. A woman who looked like her in New York City had to have some guy jumping through hoops for her. I'd taken a chance and asked if she had a significant other. The fact that I cared also surprised the hell out of me.

Mita was still waiting patiently for me to spill all the shit that was going through my mind at that moment. *How can I explain that Jada Forte is more than an attraction?*

I shook my head as if that could make the shit inside me go away. "I want to consume her. I know a lot about her, but I want to know more."

"What more do you want to know about her?" Mita asked.

Like how she looks when I suck and lick her clit. I took a deep breath to expel the dirtiness from my mind. "I don't know exactly. But I feel she runs deep."

My therapist remained composed, and not one iota of her expression gave away her thoughts. "Okay, so what about her makes you feel she runs deep?"

I grunted thoughtfully. That was the easiest question she'd asked me that day. "She's nice. No, kind. And for real, you know. She's not fucking around about how nice she is. But she's not a pushover either."

Dr. Sharma shuffled through the notebook containing all of our sessions since the first, four and a half years ago. She finally stopped at a certain point and shook her finger. "This is very interesting." She raised her head in the way she did when she was on the verge of doing some of her best shrinking. "We have already determined that your spying was the result of your curiosity but also showed an underlying feeling of hope. You were essentially on the outside looking in at what was unattainable." When she entangled her fingers on her lap, I knew we were about to go deep. "You said

Jada Forte was kind and good. Are you aware of what you're feeling when you're watching her without permission?"

"Shame." I fought the urge to drop my head. I had some new fucking tools, though. "But I know why I'm doing it."

Again, she waited silently.

"I always envisioned my real mother as the person Jada Forte is." I jerked my head back, appalled at what I was saying. I had just connected the fucking dots. "Shit, do I want to fuck my mother?"

"Then you want to have sexual relations with Miss Forte?"

I felt my eyes expand. I wasn't supposed to divulge that. *Lie*, the old me said. "Yes." I felt like choking on the truth I had just told.

Finally, she sighed, picked up her pen off her lap, and finished flipping through the pages. "So, what I'm hearing you say is a young woman has entered your space, and you are sexually attracted to her, but you've found other traits about her that you admire"—she raised a finger—"and that's the part that's foreign to you. Also, you say she's kind and good, much different from how you have previously described yourself." She looked down at her notes. "In the past, you've said that you'd never had sex with a woman you liked. You also said you found women naturally unkind and self-centered. You said it was how God made them so they could ridicule men and suck the life out of them and either not give a damn about it or ignore the fact that they were doing it." Her indifferent expression landed on me again.

Did I say that? That sure as hell sounds like me—not now but at some point.

I nodded, taking responsibility for what I'd said. She pressed her lips into a tight smile. She did that when she was sure I had done something right. It used to be difficult for me to accept accountability for my words and deeds. I used to believe the world owed me shit for hurting me, breaking my heart, and making life financially easy but loveless as hell.

"We determined that you believed your sister, Bryn, and the woman who pretended to be your mother wasn't kind or good."

I nodded sharply, smashing my lips together. She was going down a painful road, and instead of stopping her, I decided to continue with the ride.

"Spencer, we did this work during our first year

together. You already have a firm grip on the levels of judgment versus acceptance. Remember that?"

I nodded stiffly.

She sighed sharply as she narrowed an eye. "You expressed attraction to other women during our sessions in the past, but you've never been close to reverting back to old habits of skulking and spying, which was part of your behavior system from the ages of"—she frowned down at her notes —"eleven through twenty-nine." Her gaze rolled around the room. "You never told me why you came all the way to Jackson Hole, Wyoming. You said your father used to own this ranch?"

I sat up tall like a man. "I have to stop you here, Mita. You know I can't tell you why I'm in Jackson Hole. But I find our discussion very enlightening."

"And how's that?" she said, keeping her tone flat.

An era existed when I'd felt the need to push back on any woman who didn't know when enough was enough. But that was the old me, the part of myself Father had manipulated into existence.

"I had a lapse of judgment. But I understand why it happened in this place, and it does have something to do with the reason I'm here."

She shifted abruptly in her seat. "I understand,

but, Spencer, I must ask—you do remember the ritual, do you not? Stalk, seduce your partner into engaging in masochism, and then ultimately abandon her. Are you afraid that you're regressing back to acting out that behavior with Jada Forte?"

I breathed in deeply through my nose, pulling my shoulders back. "You know that it takes two consenting adults." I narrowed my eyes at her, offended. "Clear consent before I engage in that fucking behavior. Not flirting by Post-it." I told her about Jada and my back-and-forth and how hot it had gotten me. Jada wanted me, and I knew it.

Mita nodded calmly. "I understand. As a professional, I had to ask."

I turned to face the wall to my right, and I saw myself standing over Jada's bed, watching her sleep, fighting the urge to join her and the need to have her supple skin against mine. I wanted to lick every part of Jada Forte. I wanted to make her feel safe, not hurt her. I knew she would never beg me to hurt her, misuse her, and then toss her away like yesterday's trash. And I didn't want to treat her that way.

I avoided the urge to squeeze the sides of my head to relieve the pressure. Instead, I straightened in my chair, sitting strong, like a man who could have an adult reaction to a serious and valid question. "I understand."

She smiled as if satisfied and proud of my answer. "Good, Spencer. Listen, I believe you are soaring. You have the tools in your wheelhouse. You can't be perfect all the time, but the fact that you've talked about it and shared your fears with me—and answered the difficult questions pertaining to owning your feelings and behavior—lets me know that you will never hurt this woman. I also know that you are indeed ready when it comes to being in a healthy relationship, be it with friends, family, employees, or a lover." She reached over to turn off her timer, which flashed green light instead of chiming. She said the lack of sound was to not disturb any heightened emotion that could lead to awareness that may occur at the end of a session.

I wanted to thank her for believing in me. I knew I would never hurt Jada, but I still wasn't sure I deserved her.

"Just remember, Spencer, even when you doubt," she said. "You are good. You are strong. You are a kind, intelligent, and successful man, and as a human being, you have a lot to offer the world."

I didn't know about that, but if she said so, then

it had to be true. I walked her to her car, and to my fucking surprise, when we stepped out on the porch, Martin and Jada were standing there. Her big beautiful eyes shifted from my face to Mita's and then back to mine.

CHAPTER EIGHT

JADA FORTE

"Good afternoon," the beautiful woman with shiny black hair and hauntingly sexy eyes said.

"Good afternoon," I replied kindly, even though I could feel my confusion making me frown.

I wondered who she was and if she was the reason I hadn't seen him for the last two days. I tried not to stare as she walked down the steps. The woman wore a form-fitting black skirt suit, the sort that femme fatales wore in film noirs. She left a syrupy sensual sort of energy behind after each step. She was definitely Spencer Christmas's type— seductive, exotic, and probably the most beautiful woman in the world.

"Hey, keep up," Martin said. To my surprise, he turned out to be the one who'd driven me from the airport to the ranch. He was a man of few words, but his accent, quick energy, and fast gestures were straight out of the Bronx. I'd met guys like him before. They were the type who hardly left the borough, which made me wonder why Spencer had brought him to the ranch.

Spencer stepped up beside me. "Martin, I'll take her."

Martin rubbed the back of his neck. "Are you sure, boss? 'Cause I don't mind."

Spencer's frown intensified. "I said I'll take her."

There was a lot I wanted to focus on at once. The beautiful woman got behind the driver's seat of a burgundy car. Martin finished skipping down the stairs and continued along the front of the house. I tried to keep my focus on him and the car, but Spencer's energy was overwhelming me. I could hardly believe he was standing beside me even though he'd walked out of the house with another woman.

"Ready?" Spencer said loudly.

I ripped my eyes off Martin and was suddenly

unable to look away from Spencer's face. "Who was she?"

"She's business." He started down the steps with his head down. "We're taking the golf cart. Let's go."

I finished absorbing the moment and started off behind him. When I made it to the bottom of the stairs, he took my hand and guided me into the golf cart. My nerves tingled like floating glitter and rays of rainbows. Even after I quickly snatched my hand out of his, the sensation didn't stop. Somehow, in my foggy haze of attraction, I plopped myself into the front seat. It was chilly out, and my face was already turning into a flesh-sicle. My coat was nice and thick, made for New York winters, but even it wasn't keeping me warm enough. So I folded my arms and hugged myself tightly.

Spencer curved his neck to look at me as he turned on the engine. "Cold?"

I nodded jerkily.

He stabbed a button with his finger, which made doors fold down on both sides and the back. Next, he turned on the heater, and the lukewarm air blowing on me steadily increased its heat.

"Better?" he asked.

I yawned. "Better."

He paused to examine me. "You've slept well?"

I pressed my lips, trying to control my second yawn as I nodded like a bobblehead. The cart had warmed my body so comfortably that it reminded me how exhausted I was.

"But you're tired," he stated.

"I haven't really had time to chill out. Tomorrow's Saturday, though. I assume I'm off on the weekends?"

He clenched the steering wheel and pulled away from the curb. "Of course you are. You're off for the rest of the day too. I want you to get the rest you need, Jada. I never intended for you to sacrifice your health for this job."

I turned to gaze at his beautiful profile. Gosh, he was so handsome. No man in the world should have been so good-looking and weird at the same time.

"I'm fine," I said in a syrupy tone. "I'm built Forte tough."

He shook his head adamantly. "Still, you'll rest for the remainder of the day."

"But you're paying me a lot of money to stay on top of this hefty job I'm doing. And I mean, it's hefty." I immediately wanted to take back what I'd just said. I didn't want my new boss to think I was a complainer. No matter what, great mental capacity was needed to take meticulous notes during meetings while recording everyone's concerns and questions and researching information to attach to summaries so that my boss could respond to his colleagues effectively. It was draining. As long as I did the job he'd hired me to do, I would be exhausted.

Spencer's frown intensified. "I know."

We fell silent. I wondered what he was thinking, and if I'd been in a real relationship with him, I would have asked. I wished I weren't so exhausted and could enjoy the exhilaration of sitting so close to him in such a small and contained environment.

Finally, he cleared his throat. "Just as an FYI, you're not allowed to go roaming wherever you want. The atrium will have everything you need."

I turned to take in the fields of wild grass and dark mountains rising in the distance. I was pretty sure he didn't have to worry about me wandering off. "What about town? I may need to get some essentials."

"Write a list of everything you'll need, and Felix will take care of it for you."

I whipped my attention to his perfect profile and

blinked at him. He continued looking straight ahead.

"What if I want to go into town to get people contact?"

"As long as you're here, you stay here."

I shook my head jerkily. "Is that your round-about way of saying that I can't leave the property?"

His Adam's apple bobbed. "You have every-thing you need here, Jada."

"But not people contact. Not a social life," I whined.

He glanced at me, and it was long enough for his glare to burn me through and through. "You can't leave the property. That's the rule."

I threw my hands up. "Then I'm a prisoner?" I was being purposely dramatic.

"You're not a prisoner, Jada. You may leave at any time. However, while you work for me, you stay on this property." His even tone had a sharpness to it that could cut through steel. *Why do I find that so damn sexy?*

He sighed forcefully. "I don't want you to leave. I understand you're lonely, and I will do a better job of being present. Sarah works in the atrium. She'll provide you with company as long as you're there."

I almost wanted to laugh my head off, but after taking a second look at him, I saw he was being serious. I slumped as I narrowed my eyes at a large building that resembled a ski lodge coming up on my right. "You're the boss, and I need the money," I muttered.

He didn't respond, but I could feel him watching me. I refused to meet his gaze.

"Did you see how we got here?" he finally asked.

"Yes." I kept my eyes off him. He knew I wasn't an idiot. The atrium was less than a mile up the road from the main house.

"This cart will be yours. You can drive it to the atrium whenever you want. It'll remained parked in the front of the house for you."

When I finally turned, our eyes connected. I saw the tiny flecks of light brown in his blue irises. I had to rip my attention from the strange moment we were sharing. I heard his door open and close, and soon he was on my side, opening my door for me.

I felt as if I was walking on air as I followed him up the path to our destination. When we made it to the entrance, he held the door open for me, and once again, I felt giddy as I passed him. As soon as I stepped inside, the warmth and moisture from the

Olympic-sized Roman-styled swimming pool filled the air.

"Wow, this is nice," I said.

I turned to make sure Spencer was there. He was standing still, watching me with a burning look in his eyes. A knot formed at the bottom of my throat as shivers of excitement raced through me. The desirous energy he emitted enslaved me. The moist air stood still as I watched him reach down for my hand. *Is this a dream?* Then our bodies were pressing against each other. His chest was hard, his hands strong, and the bulge between his legs made of steel.

"Mr. Christmas, it's you," a woman said happily.

He quickly let go of me as we turned to see a young woman who looked to be in her early twenties. She was wearing tight black yoga pants that hugged her crotch and a white fitted T-shirt, knotted to display her midriff. Her hair was in a ponytail that swung as she pranced our way, and she seemed confused about whether to settle her curious but friendly gaze on Spencer or me.

"You must be Jada Forte," she said, keeping a smile pinned to her lips.

I wasn't shocked that she was aware of my

arrival. I was getting the impression that everyone I'd come in contact with had not only been hand-picked to be here, but had been instructed to make me comfortable. I walked up to her and shook her clammy hand.

"Yep, that's me," I said cheerfully.

"I'm Sarah."

Suddenly, I heard the door open. I whipped my head around, but it had closed. Spencer was gone.

───────────

SARAH WAS AN UPBEAT PERSON WHOSE JOB IT WAS TO maintain the atrium. She kept a high-pitched, optimistic tone as she pointed out the Jacuzzi, steam room, and sauna. She showed me where I could have facials and massages—but I had to schedule the sessions in advance so a clinician could be flown in.

"Has everyone who works on the ranch been flown in?" I asked as we stood behind the counter in a cozy room that looked like an upscale spa.

Sarah responded by not changing her smile, which by now I knew was as practiced as her peppiness. It was her job to be a cordial host. I wondered how much Spencer was paying her and whether sex was included with her salary.

"I don't know, but we'll have someone here this weekend, so you can just schedule your massage and facial with no worries," Sarah said.

I took note of her glossed-over answer. I could have insisted we have a longer discussion about it, but I wasn't in the business of shaking down other employees to obtain information just to soothe my curiosity, so I shrugged, letting it go. "Sure, why not."

"Okay," she sang. "Morning or afternoon?"

"Afternoon."

"Afternoon, it is!" She reached under the counter, brought out a clipboard, and wrote my name on one of the lines. But I didn't miss that Spencer Christmas also had been scheduled for a massage at one o'clock on Saturday and Sunday. I found myself wondering if Sarah was the one who was going to give it to him, complete with a happy ending. If so, I certainly didn't want to be around to see the aftereffects. I changed my mind and asked for the morning.

I could have stayed and gone for a swim, but I really wanted to get back to the house and veg out in my stunning bedroom. When I walked outside, I longed to find Spencer waiting for me behind the wheel of the golf cart, but he wasn't there. If I was given another opportunity to be trapped in the cart with him, I would question him about his relationship with Sarah. I was sure they were fucking.

There, mystery solved. I slid into the driver's seat of the golf cart and turned the key, which was already in the ignition. Now I knew who he was having sex with and why he wasn't attempting to do it with me.

When I made it back to the house, I learned that Spencer had already given Marta instructions to set me up for lunch in my bedroom. She asked if I was okay with shrimp ravioli with a fresh antipasto salad and an assortment of cannolis for dessert. I dragged my tired body up the steps, only remembering when I'd made it halfway up that I could have taken the elevator. I was distracted by memories of being in Spencer's embrace. *What was that? What was he about to do—kiss me?*

When I entered my room, I fell onto the bed

and tried to fantasize about how it would feel to have Spencer's lips on mine and his tongue in my mouth. I saw us go at it, hot and heavy, Spencer groping my tits and licking up the side of my neck like this guy I made out with had done once. I liked it—I thought it was freaky and erotic. When that guy from the past tried to run his hand down my pants after doing that, I'd grabbed his wrist and rolled out from under him, scooting off the bed. But when the Spencer in my fantasy did it, I asked him to take me but be gentle, please, because it was my first time.

The ringing doorbell jolted me out of my thoughts. I sat up straight, my eyes popping open. I pressed a hand over my heart to steady myself. Once I was calm, I called, "Come in."

One of the servers asked if I would like to have my lunch upstairs or downstairs. I chose upstairs, since I intended to lie in bed and binge read *The Dark Christmases*.

A pair of men rolled a silver cart to the round table with two chairs beyond the foot of my bed. The aroma of the food made me clench my stomach. I couldn't wait to dive in. Curious, I watched them arrange two plates. Two glasses. Two sets of silverware. A basket of bread. Beverage service.

I waved for them to stop. "You don't have to set two place settings. It's just me."

"I'll be joining you," Spencer said from behind me.

I turned to see him, in all his glory, standing in the doorway.

CHAPTER NINE

JADA FORTE

A new word for *awkward* needed to be invented as we sat across from each other, eating in silence. The sexual tension between us felt as if it was going to zap all the life out of me. We kept trying to avoid eye contact. Then we both took a drink of water at the same time. We smiled at each other.

"Sorry. I'm not a very good conversationalist," he said.

I frowned and nodded thoughtfully, stitching together all the conversations we'd ever had. "I guess you're right," I finally concluded.

His eyebrows wrinkled then smoothed.

"So," I said, feeling naughty. "Are you saying you want to have a real conversation with me?"

His mouth lifted into the sexiest smirk I'd ever seen. "Why not?" He readjusted in his seat, crossing his legs, and looked at me as if daring me to bring it.

I knew exactly the topic he wanted to discuss. "Okay, so you said that beautiful woman who was here earlier was 'business.'" I turned my head. "What sort of business?"

I thought he would wipe the smirk off his face, but he didn't. "The nature of the business is between me and her."

"Was it sex?" *Holy shit! I can't believe I asked that.* I couldn't even look him in the eye, and the fact that I couldn't walk that question back made me want to disappear into the firm cushions of my chair.

Spencer cleared his throat. "Have you ever had sex, Jada?"

I felt my eyes grow wide. He asked that with such ease, while I was secretly freaking out. For sure, I'd stopped breathing, so I inhaled deeply to get the process going again.

"Huh?" I said, the word coming out strained.

"Never mind." He uncrossed his legs. "No, there is no sex between me and her."

I pressed my lips, blinking rapidly. I was now more than happy to let any conversation involving sex fizzle away. *But why did he ask if I was a virgin? Can he smell it on me? See it in my eyes?* The woman he'd walked out of the house with earlier that day had probably had a lot of good sex. Spencer might have business with her, but based on the ease with which they shared each other's company, they must have had an intimate bond as well.

"So, do you have any brothers or sisters?" he asked.

My attention had wandered off, so I set my focus back on him. "No. I'm an only child."

His eyebrows furrowed as if he hadn't believed me.

"Well, I am," I said, sounding more defensive than I would have liked.

Spencer evened out his expression. "I see. How long have your parents been married?"

I tilted my head. "I thought you knew everything about me."

He cut a smirk. "I'm asking about your parents, not you."

I had a pithy reply prepared, but I was too hypnotized by the way his lips lifted ever so slightly into that sexy smirk. It took a minute to register what he'd said. "Oh, my parents. Right. They've been married for thirty-one years."

Spencer's grunt was filled with intrigue.

"What?" I asked.

"Nothing. Good for them. So, Jada…"

He had my complete attention as I chewed on the most delicious ravioli I'd ever tasted. "Huh?" I finally said because his pause was too lengthy.

"How does a woman who looks like you have no boyfriend?"

I felt as though my head was floating away from my body. "You think I'm attractive."

He cocked his head curiously. "Don't you?"

I pressed my hand on my chest. "Do I think I'm attractive?"

He nodded gently. Gosh, he looked so sexy when he did that.

"Um, well… I'm not lacking in self-esteem. But…" It felt weird talking about how I looked and, especially, articulating it to him.

"But…?"

"But I don't go out of my way to appeal to the opposite sex." I thought of how I'd been dolling myself up since I arrived. I'd never before taken so much time to apply mascara, blush, and lipstick. I crossed and uncrossed my legs. "I mean, it depends."

"On what?"

I looked up and away from my lap. "If I'm going out with friends or…" I gazed at his waiting expression and shrugged nonchalantly. "Work." My voice cracked, so I cleared my throat.

His eyes seemed to search my face. "So, you've been in public relations for six years?"

Relieved he was changing the subject, I smirked. "For someone who's not conversational, you sure are good at it."

I made him smirk again, and it felt like a gift from the Almighty.

"Do you like your work?"

I nodded thoughtfully. "I do. I really do."

"You ever thought about entering into politics?" He put food in his mouth and chewed as he waited for an answer. His sexy lips were distracting.

I cleared my throat. "Not if I have to work with my mom. And let's face it, everyone from the president to the lowest member in Congress has to deal with Senator Patricia Forte at some point."

Spencer Christmas remained very still as he observed me. "Do you disagree with her politically?"

I shrugged. "Sometimes I do, and sometimes I don't. I never allow any person or ideal to put me in a box."

My skin warmed as he studied me with a soft expression.

I cleared my throat. "And you've been in finance for how long?" I asked, my voice at least two octaves too high.

Spencer Christmas looked off thoughtfully. "A long time."

"Do you like it?"

"I don't know." His burning gaze was back on me.

He had my rapt attention. "Why not?" I waited for his reply with bated breath.

"Maybe because it was what was expected of me."

I grunted thoughtfully. "I guess I know how that feels."

Again, we were staring into each other's eyes.

"So, Jada…"

I was feeling the full force of his gaze. "Yes," I chirped and then cleared the nervousness out of my throat. "I mean, yes." I tried to sound more confident the second time but didn't succeed. He'd had made me nervous and horny as hell just by saying my name that way.

He raised an eyebrow. "Are you really a virgin?"

Every muscle in my body stiffened. I hadn't

expected him to ask that again. However, I was more in control of my wits this time. I folded in my arms across my chest. "Are you a virgin?"

He grinned naughtily. "That depends on how we want to look at it."

I could feel the warm wetness drenching my panties. Every time I interacted with him, I got wet. If he were around more, I'd run out of panties faster. "What do you mean by that?"

Spencer Christmas turned to look at my bed, and so did I. I wondered if this was his way of offering to de-virgin me. Then he set his attention back on me. "A man lives in phases."

My mouth had been caught open, so I closed it to swallow. "What do you mean by that?" I whispered.

He moved his mouth as if he wanted to say more but then clamped his lips together and stood abruptly. I jumped, startled.

"Jada, stand," he said with his hand stretched out toward me.

I could hear myself breathe and felt jitters race through me. Even though I was nervous as hell, I did what he had asked and took his hand. Once I was standing, Spencer Christmas guided me against him. I nearly crumpled in his arms as I felt the stiffness in his groan. I'd been this close to a hard cock many times before. I've even let a couple of guys rub one out on me. However, none of their penises had felt as dense as Spencer's.

"It's been a long time since a woman has gotten me like this," he whispered, his warm breath pressing against my ear. "If I had known you were so fucking sexy, I never would've hired you."

I gasped when he ground his healthy erection against me. Our gazes latched on to each other and refused to let go. *What next, Jada?* I tried desperately to make myself come to my senses. The hard truth that I had to admit was that I was completely under Spencer Christmas's control. He could do whatever the hell he wanted to me. I felt my eyes expand when his lips moved closer to mine. But then, to my dismay, he jerked his head away and then let go of me as he took a step back.

We still couldn't take our eyes off each other. However, I could see disappointment and shock in his. I wanted to say something. I was good at bringing moments like this back to a space where both people involved could laugh about them or pretend they'd never happened.

I was still trying to come up with words when suddenly, Spencer turned, leaving me looking at the back of his head. I wanted to ask where he was going, but after what had just transpired, I knew we couldn't just continue with lunch as though the sexual tension wasn't too intense for us to ignore. The muscles in my body remained tight until he closed the door behind him.

When he was gone, my legs felt as though they'd turned to jelly. I quickly calculated the distance between my abandoned chair and the foot of my bed. The chair was closer, so I made my way to it and plopped down on the seat. I was very clear on what I needed to do next. The time had come for me to dive into *The Dark Christmases*.

CHAPTER TEN

JADA FORTE

I read through the rest of lunch, even when the servers came and carted out the dirty dishes and uneaten food. Then I asked if they could serve me dinner in my room. Once again, I told them I'd have what Mr. Christmas was having.

"He won't be dining in tonight," the server said.

I smiled gently, masking my disappointment. "That's fine. Then tell the chef to be creative. I'll eat whatever's put before me."

The server bowed his head.

"One more thing," I said, raising my finger. "Could I get a bottle of red wine?"

"Yes, Jada."

The staff even had a formal way of saying, "Jada." It would have sounded natural for the server to just refer to me as Miss Forte, but it was too late to quack about it. I probably shouldn't have complained about what the house staff called me in the first place. It was totally a Patricia Forte move—trying to make people feel I was down to earth and having no concept that the very act of getting them to call me what was more comfortable to me was entitled behavior.

When he was gone, I moved from the armchair to lie across the bed and read on. First of all, I learned the lineage of the Christmases. They went way back to some of the oldest American money. They'd been lucky enough to come to the United States with a chest that would allow them a leg up on others who arrived in the 1800s. The book went into all the industries they invested in as well as the marriages and children.

Luther Peter Christmas had three daughters and four sons, but he spent most of his waking hours working and his nights at brothels. He would only come home to knock up his wife Rosemary Louise Christmas, who was very depressed and was eventually diagnosed with hysteria. Rosemary had spent her final years in an insane asylum. Upon her deathbed, she said that her years in captivity had been the happiest of her life.

The doorbell rang, drawing my attention out of the pages, and the server brought in my bottle of wine along with a long-stemmed glass. I thanked him for fulfilling my request, and once he was gone, I poured myself a glass, undressed, put on my spaghetti-strapped night dress, and started reading again.

Randolph Wesley Christmas, Spencer's father, was Luther's great-grandson. Randolph's father, James Randolph Bartholomew Christmas, had seven wives, all more than twenty years younger than he was. Three of them died of the flu, and the other three, who never bore him any children, simply walked out on him and took nothing with them. He was said to have been a severe, unloving man. The stepmothers and mothers behaved as if the children never existed.

I was at the part where Randolph met Amelia at an event held in honor of her father. And then the story began to unfold.

"Holy fuck," I said after reading halfway through.

I had to pour myself another glass of wine and read it again. Yes, I'd read it right. Amelia had been thirteen years old and Randolph Christmas pushing fifty. What the book recounted next made my jaw hit the floor.

I was seriously deep into some messed-up shit when the doorbell rang and the servers brought dinner and another bottle of wine. I couldn't pull my nose out of the pages as they set up.

"Would you like me to tell you what's being served tonight?" the server asked.

I forced my eyes away from a haunting description of the construction of the Christmas manor. I smiled impatiently. "No, thank you."

"All right, then," he said with a nod. "We'll collect the dishes when you call."

"Thank you." I went right back to reading. I didn't even wait until he'd left.

The construction of the Christmas mansion was fascinating, to say the least. And Holly Henderson sure as hell knew how to make a mundane topic exciting. She talked about the blueprints and how Mr. Christmas had carefully designed every inch of the property. She explained the rooms—the feel of each and the supposed intention behind it. Then she progressed into the secret hallways and how they connected throughout the mansion. I felt as if I was trapped in a crypt with the Christmases.

I'd finished my second big glass of Bordeaux

red and was on my third. I'd never drunk that much in my life, but the wine was good, and so was the book. Before long, the book took an even darker turn. It started with the life of Jasper Walker Christmas, the oldest. Terrible and harsh things had happened to the boy, all in the name of grooming him to take over the empire. He'd been exposed to a lot of lasciviousness—he watched women and men provide pleasures to businessmen his father wanted to coerce. Then there was the torture. My heart could hardly take the acts visited upon the young Jasper Christmas. That part was written so graphically that I couldn't keep myself from feeling all the pain visited upon him. However, I also experienced the young man's determination to get through it. I felt his mother, Amelia Christmas, who was a very complex individual, strengthen him both physically and mentally. The strange thing was that I also felt that she was more than a mother to him in many ways—she was his lover without the sex. It was weird, gross, and necessary all at the same time —the way she would steal into his room in the middle of the night and watch him sleep and the way he would do the same with her. The book didn't say what Amelia was thinking as she watched her son in the dark, but it showed her as being very different from the prostitutes her husband dragged through the tunnels and into his sex den on the third floor of the mansion.

The next chapter was about Spencer Hunter Christmas, and by then, I could hardly keep my eyes open, even though there was no way I could close them either. If I hadn't been so tired, I might have managed to sweep through the entire 453-page book in fewer than twenty-four hours. No wonder it was still on the best-seller list after being in print for five years. I wondered how I had just discovered it.

I started the pages about Spencer, reading about how lonely he'd been as a little boy and how he used to get in trouble, hoping his father would punish him the way he did Jasper. But it never worked. He might as well have not existed as far as Randolph Christmas was concerned. When Spencer tried to draw Amelia's attention, she didn't ignore him, but she wasn't much of a mother either. She wasn't mean to him, but he wished she would be. Spencer would try to rattle Amelia to get her to hit him, kick him, or tell him to get the hell away from her. He went to college when he was seventeen, and when he returned, she finally showed him the attention he'd longed for.

My heart had sunk to the depths of my belly when the account ended, promising to pick up later in the book. I wanted to know more about what had happened between Spencer and Amelia, but first, I had to read about the twins, Asher and Bronwyn. I really wanted to skip that part and get right to Spencer, but I also wanted to savor the entire book in its proper order.

Either way, I couldn't go on. I rubbed my eyes. My brain was spent and my sight blurry from focusing on the screen for far too long. I checked the time before pressing the button on the side of my device. It was after two o'clock in the morning. I wondered if Spencer had returned from wherever he'd gone for dinner. I found myself wishing he would come check in on me. I also wanted to ask if, when he came home from college, Amelia Christmas had given him the attention he'd always sought. But I didn't want to let him know I'd been reading the book. He hadn't wanted me to read it, and maybe he'd fire me if he knew I was gripped by its pages.

I pressed the button on the side of my device, and the screen went black. I got up to lift the silver covers from over the porcelain plates and inspect dinner. The crab cakes were huge, and the seafood salad contained succulent shrimp, crab, and fish meat. I put my finger on top of a crab cake to test the temperature of it—there was hardly anything more awful than eating a cold one. It was still warm, so I dug in, and before I knew it, all the food on my dinner and salad plates—including dessert—was gone. I was hungrier than I'd realized, and I couldn't ignore the spinning in my head. I was tipsy. My inhibitions were crushed, and I wondered if I should go on a search for Spencer's room. As I took steps toward the door, I could barely walk, so instead, I turned off the light and kept walking until I collapsed on the bed.

CHAPTER ELEVEN

JADA FORTE

"Jada?" There was a pause. "Jada?"

I felt myself being shaken, and slowly, I began to wake from a dream I'd already forgotten. Darkness surrounded me. The man said my name again, and then I perceived that I wasn't alone in my bedroom. Fright took hold of me, and I scrambled to sit up against the massive headboard.

"It's me," he said. His voice was quiet and tempered by a hint of vulnerability.

I pressed my hand over my beating chest as I continued blinking to better my focus. In the dark, and standing beside my bed, was the tall and fit frame of Spencer Christmas. He was shirtless, and his bare chest glistened in the moonlight that flooded in through the windows.

"What are you doing here?" I asked. I wasn't sure how I felt about him standing in my room, clearly uninvited, while I was sleeping.

"Should I leave?"

I frowned, contemplating his question. Suddenly, I became self-aware, wondering how I looked. I'd drunk a lot of wine before falling asleep, and my mind was still loopy. As a matter of fact, I wasn't even sure that what seemed to be happening was actually happening.

"Are you…?" I started and then gained a better focus on him. Instead of pinching myself, I rubbed my arm, and the feeling on my skin proved that the moment was real.

"I couldn't sleep without…"

I watched him with tired eyes, waiting for him to finish. Then, without warning, Spencer Christmas's face was moving toward mine until our lips touched. A whimper escaped me as he slid his tongue into my mouth. I closed my eyes to inhale his scent. His mouth tasted strongly of wine and mint. Spencer Christmas had prepared for this kiss. The deeper our tongues explored each other and our lips caressed, the more I felt as if I was having an out-of-body experience.

"Jada," he whispered as his hand slid up the middle of my thighs, parting my legs as it traveled to my drenched pussy. "Umm," he moaned, sinking his fingers inside me.

I thrust my head back onto the pillow. I'd had guys finger-fuck me before, but Spencer was rubbing me in spots that had never been stimulated.

"You like how that feels," he whispered.

I clung tightly to his strong forearm, squeezing the life out of it as he continued rubbing me there. *What in the hell is he doing?*

"Ooh, Jada," he whispered.

Oh shit. I squeezed my eyes shut as the sensation gathered steam.

"Jada," he called louder and with authority.

I wanted to answer, but all I could do was whimper. If only he would stop, take a break. Then I would be able to say, "Yes, Spencer." But he remained unrelenting.

I heard myself scream. I felt my body wriggle, and the strongest orgasm ever pulsed through my pussy. The pleasure lasted longer than usual. Spencer's warm mouth was now down there. I could feel his breath cooling my wetness and his tongue inside me. With that erotic sensation, the buildup began again.

"Spencer," I said with a sigh, struggling to lift my head and see what he was doing. But the orgasmic feeling was overpowering my desire to see. I screamed again as more pleasure spread through my pussy like a flower opening its petals under the sun.

Spencer slid on top above me, straddling me as he wrapped his long fingers around my delicate wrists and held them to the bed. He watched me firmly, swallowing hard, and then his lips parted. I had a strong desire to erase the distance between our mouths and bodies. But he remained where he was, watching. I could tell he was thinking I was too far away. Fear, longing, and surrender tempered my very being.

"Can I have you?" he said, his voice promising joyous passion.

I could feel my heart beating at the back of my throat. I nodded, swallowing nervously. This was it. This was how it was going to happen.

Spencer Christmas raised his eyebrows. "Yes or no?"

A force stronger than me wanted to take over

my mouth and shout the answer, but instead, I breathily said, "Yes."

"This is your first time?"

I nodded again.

"I'm going to make it pleasurable for you, Jada."

My lips parted, and instead of speaking, I sucked air as my body recalled exactly what he'd just done to it. I wondered how he could make it more pleasurable than that.

"Do you want your first time to be enjoyable, baby?"

The lust in his expression was driving me crazy. Still unable to speak, I nodded enthusiastically.

"Say yes," he commanded.

My body stiffened, pussy weeping for him. "Yes," I said with a sigh, my body twisting with longing.

Suddenly, Spencer stood and walked away from me.

I propped myself up on my forearms. "Where are you going?" I prayed he wasn't playing power games, getting me all hot and bothered and then abandoning me. That was certainly his style.

"Stay there, and lie down," he ordered.

His voice was forceful. Normally, I would have

wanted to rebel against anyone who took that tone with me, but I quickly pinched my head against my pillow, turned on in the extreme.

I could hear him fiddling around at the table. When he walked back to me, he was holding something. I watched him step out of his sweatpants and underwear. When he stood again, his erection shot out like a missile. The sheer size and girth of his engorged cock made my eyes expand. *Holy shit. Is he planning on putting that thing in me?*

Fear overcame me, but I didn't want to call it off. He said it wouldn't hurt, but I doubted that. However, as long as my first lover was Spencer Christmas, I was ready for the pain.

"Spread your legs," he ordered.

I did it, watching him, feeling intoxicated with expectation.

He inhaled sharply between his clenched teeth as he stared, dazed, at my pussy. "You're so fucking wet," he whispered.

I moaned as he slipped fingers in and out of my moisture. The device in his other hand made a noise. Through my cloudy vision, I could see it was a vibrator. I faintly wondered if that was how he was planning on fucking me. I'd never slid my vibrator all the way inside my pussy. Maybe he was going to let the sex toy get me ready to receive his hefty cock. I didn't ask if that was his intention as he tugged me by my thighs until my ass was at the edge of the bed.

"Wrap your legs around me."

I did as I was told, wishing he'd turned on a light so I could see his face better. The vibrator was playing around my clit, going up and down, stimulating the same spot. The pleasure was so powerful that all I could do was surrender while forcing the back of my head into the mattress and allow whatever he was doing to happen.

"I can't wait to eat your tits," he said, still playing with my pussy with the device.

I wanted to say, "Me neither," but instead, I whimpered and sighed as an orgasm expanded through my pussy.

"Ha!" I cried, feeling pressure against the entrance of my vag. *Shit*, I could feel him still inside me. The sound of the vibrator slowed as he put it on the opposite side of my clit. I'd played with my vibrator many times and had never done anything like what he was doing. *Holy shit!* I gritted my teeth as the promise of a powerful orgasm pulsed through my pussy. Along with it came more pressure, intermixing pleasure with burning. I didn't know whether to groan in discomfort or whimper because it felt so damn good.

Spencer grunted. "Shit, you feel so good. I just want to slam my cock deep inside you, baby."

With the vibrator stimulating me, I wriggled and moaned as a new orgasm built. Soon, I screamed, climaxing. The burn was back, the two sensations intermingling again. My pussy felt stretched by Spencer's fullness.

"Take off your shirt," he whispered and then tossed his head back, sucking air in through his teeth. "I can feel you, baby. Shit, I can feel you."

The vibrator was working another part of my clit as I slipped my nightshirt off over my head. Spencer looked tortured as he intently watched what he was doing with my pussy.

"Shit," I said with a sigh as an orgasm was impending.

Then the burning was in unison with my new orgasm. I felt pleasure and pain conspiring. Slowly, indulgently, he slid his big dick in and out of me as I breathed hard, feeling the minor burn of his fullness.

Zzzz… *blop*. I heard the vibrator hit the bed. Spencer had two full hands on my ass and was jerking me slowly against his dick. "Fuck," he kept repeating. "I can feel it. I can fucking feel it!"

I could feel it, too, every single variation of his strokes. He rounded his hips, and his cock did circles in my pussy. I thought I would die of satisfaction as he shifted fast and then slower, pulling the tip of his dick to the rim of my pussy and stimulating the spots just around the entrance as he moved his thumb around my clit. He was like a masterful musician, playing my body like an instrument. I moaned and tried to twist my lower half away from his pleasurable assault to find at least a few seconds of reprieve, but Spencer's grasp was too strong. He wouldn't let me go. All I could do was moan and whimper until I cried out in ecstasy. Then he slammed his dick deep inside me again. My body jolted against the mattress as he grunted and cried out for the Almighty.

I didn't stop riding the mattress until he tilted his back and shouted, "Fuck!" as his body jerked and shivered from orgasm.

WE EXISTED IN A MOMENT FROZEN IN TIME. Spencer still had hold of my ass, and his cock was still inside me. Our gazes were glued to each other. I wanted to forever remember the afterglow of being deflowered and the sexy Adonis I'd given my virginity to.

"How was your first time?" he asked, smirking, his eyes bright and glossy.

"It was…" I searched for words better than the ones already in existence. "Perfect" was all I could come up with.

He slowly pulled himself out of me. "It was the same for me." Spencer took my thighs and carefully spun me until my legs were on the bed. He then pressed my knees together. "Don't move," he said then walked away.

I was still wet between the legs as I twisted my body on top of the bed, bathing in the exhilaration of what had just happened between us. Water ran in the bathroom, and a few minutes later, Spencer spread my legs again, and a warm towel was gently wiping my slit.

"I wore a condom," he said.

I was glad one of us remembered to be responsible.

"I've had all my tests. I have no diseases. Jada, I want to fuck you without a condom soon. You're not on the pill, are you?" He walked over to put the towel on the small table.

I wondered if I was supposed to answer that question. "Um, no, I'm not."

Surprisingly, Spencer lay down beside me. "Lie on your back."

Again, I hopped to fulfill his command, and once I was on my back, he was pinching my nipples. I winced from the stinging, but I didn't complain. He had fucked me, making pain pleasurable. I felt I owed him this.

He squeezed tighter and tighter. Only when I closed my eyes tightly and grunted at the agony did he let go and roll on top of me to sink his soft hot mouth over the sting. Spencer sucked my nipple, brushing the tip gently with his teeth. It felt so good that I wanted him to do it forever. Then he did the same to my other nipple, making it hurt then bringing it relief with mind-blowing pleasure.

"It feels so good," I whispered, my body tightening and pussy tingling.

"Don't talk."

I loved how easily I wanted to obey his commands. Obedience meant he would reward me with more sex, more orgasms, and more of him. If I couldn't speak, then I wanted to touch him everywhere. I ran my fingers through his hair, and he quickly seized my wrists and pressed my hands down on the bed. The force and that look in his eyes turned me on. The lights were still off, but the longer I stared at him, the better view I had of his sexy blues, which were so vibrant they made my pussy cream.

"What are you doing to me?" he whispered, and his mouth came crashing down on mine.

Our tongues dove deep, swirling around each other, our lips attempting to merge into one. The longer we kissed, the more I craved him, whimpering like a newborn puppy, and soon enough, he was making the same noises. I wondered if his heart felt the same as mine. I wondered if it wanted to burst into a million blazing pieces and whether his soul wanted to capture mine and hold me inside of him forever. The emotions were too intense.

Perhaps that was why Spencer abruptly stopped kissing me. His body abandoned mine, and the air from the room washed over my sweat-glistened skin.

"What is it?" I asked, watching him putting on his underwear and sweatpants.

"I have to go," he muttered.

"But why?" I whined.

"Get some sleep, Jada," he ordered. But his tone

lacked the tenderness and sexiness of his earlier commands.

I didn't know what to say. My body was starving for more of him. I could have made love until the sun rose, set, and rose again.

"But I don't want you to leave," I said.

I was instantly annoyed by my own gluttony. Spencer took a few steps toward the bathroom before correcting his course and walking toward the door, careful not to look at me. I knew there was nothing I could say to make him stay. The door creaked as it opened.

"Sleep well," he whispered soulfully and disappeared into the hallway.

I sat with my back against the headboard, wondering what in the world had happened. Something changed. I'd seen it in his eyes. I wanted to go back and replay every second of our sex, but my brain was too burnt out.

I yawned. My body was so fulfilled, and I could still smell Spencer all over my skin and taste him in my mouth. Maybe his leaving was good after all. If he'd stayed, I would have overdosed on him. I could see myself being one of those clingy girls who got fucked really hard and then believed they were in love with the guys who'd fucked them. That wouldn't be me. No way. Spencer Christmas could fuck like someone who wasn't even a human being—more like Zeus or someone—but I could never forget that he was strange and unpredictable. I pulled the covers up to my neck and settled myself comfortably in bed. My vag felt stretched and was still burning from the new experience of being fucked. I curled onto my side, feeling satisfied by the sensation. Yawning again, I closed my eyes. I wanted to call him a dick and hear myself say it, but instead, intoxication from the wine and from giving my virginity to Spencer—along with pure exhaustion —carried me off to sleep before I could muster the energy.

LOTS OF CRAZY THINGS WERE HAPPENING. I WAS racing Spencer Christmas to a lake after he told me he didn't want me swimming in it. He was winning, but I was close on his heels. Then he was kissing and embracing Sarah while laughing at me, telling her that he'd never touched me. I was standing there, watching them, sad that he was lying about what we'd done but too hurt to say anything. Next, we were in the office. He towered over me as I sat at my desk.

"I don't want you, Jada. I fucked you, and now it's over, got it?"

Tears in my eyes, I nodded feverishly.

Then he threw hundred-dollar bills on top of my desk, one after the other. "You want the money? Here's your fucking salary!"

I gasped as I woke up. I looked around the bright room and gasped again when I found Spencer sitting in the chair, staring at me.

"You," I said weakly and rubbed my eyes for better focus.

He sat up straight. "You've been asleep for a day and a half."

I rubbed the back of my neck. It was stiff. "Really?"

"Yes."

"Jeez, a day and a half? I must've been really tired," I whispered, eyeing him.

My gaze then fell on the little round table. It had been cleared. Or perhaps there had never been any dirty dishes on it. Maybe I'd never drunk too much wine. Maybe Spencer never woke me up in the middle of the night and took my virginity in the most incredible fashion.

"I'm sorry, but did we... you know?" I asked, my finger shifting between us.

He scowled. "You don't remember?" He sounded offended.

There was my answer. *Shit.* We had actually fucked. I pressed my hands over my face and fell back on top of the bed. "I remember it."

I heard him get out of the seat, and suddenly, he was above me, straddling me, fully clothed in his standard cargo pants and sweatshirt. I felt he was being careful to keep his body off mine.

"If you were questioning whether or not we fucked, then maybe I didn't do a good enough job."

I gulped. I wanted to say something, but his face was too close to mine. This wasn't the movies. I had the worst morning breath, and I sure as hell didn't want him getting a whiff of it.

Spencer studied me with his customary scowl before rising to his feet. "Have brunch in the dining room. The maids will come change your sheets and tidy up while you're eating."

I curled my shoulders vulnerably, pulling the comforter closer to my neck. "Will you be joining me?"

Again, he watched me, frowning, and I

wondered what in the world he was thinking. "No," he said curtly. "Not for breakfast."

I did the calculations in my mind. "Is today Sunday?"

Spencer walked toward the door. "Yes."

Before I could ask him another question, he was gone. The guy had a poetic way of exiting a room that really sucked. I shook my head and once again questioned whether we'd actually had sex.

I raised the duvet and saw the red on the white sheets. "Shit, cherry popped."

I fell back on the bed, pulled the covers over my head, and groaned.

CHAPTER TWELVE

JADA FORTE

I wondered where I had put my cellphone as I pondered calling Hope and filling her in on what had happened between my new boss and me. Then I tried to imagine what I should call him—Mr. Christmas or Spencer. Perhaps it depended on the activity. Mr. Christmas for work and Spencer for play.

Play? I doubted we would have sex again. That thought made me want to cry. I told myself that the last dream I'd had about him had more to do with my fears than any premonition. Hope would always say that I'd remained single because I had the Prince Charming complex, meaning if a guy wasn't darn near wooing me like a prince in a fairy tale, then I couldn't trust that he was fully into me. And if I couldn't trust him, then I could easily write him off. I'd never understood how her assessment applied to me until that moment.

"For goodness's sake, Jada," I whispered.

He'd been sitting in a chair, watching me, when I woke up. I wondered how long he'd been there. *Goodness gracious*—he was so hard to read, and I was good at reading people. He was just a constant enigma.

If it weren't for the fact that I was starving, I would have lain in bed a little longer. But it was time to get back to real life. I decided to return to my room after breakfast and pick up where I left off reading *The Dark Christmases*.

On that note, I walked carefully to the shower and set the water at a comfortable temperature. I'd brought my own shampoo, but there was a pretty expensive brand already on the shelf, so I used that instead.

While lathering my hair, I worked very hard to recall every detail of Spencer and my lovemaking. He'd said a lot that night, but I could hardly remember any of it. For instance, he'd kept repeating something while thrusting his cock in and out of me, but I couldn't remember what it was.

Steam rose all around me as the water hit my

face. The warmth felt good. Then, out of nowhere, I felt a hard body against my back.

"I couldn't stay away," Spencer whispered.

His rigid shaft slid up the crease of my ass, and he moaned in my ear before doing it again. I had to blink twice to make sure this was happening.

Spencer spun me around to face him. I inhaled sharply as our gazes met. He brushed one of his dry cheeks against my wet one, and then he did the other side before his lips connected with mine, teasing them with tender kisses. My head spun, and I quivered in his embrace. Thank goodness I had rinsed the sour taste out of my mouth while washing my hair.

Our kissing turned more vigorous. Spencer's lips and tongue sought to consume mine. His fingers dug into me as he nearly lifted me off the floor to kiss me deeper. I moaned as my pussy began to flutter. He shoved his hand between my legs and finger-banged me, releasing a deep breath.

Without any warning, he lifted me off my feet. I felt as light as a leaf in his clutches as he walked me to the large shower bench. I couldn't take my eyes off his face. His expression was eager as he parted my thighs, and he watched me carefully as he set me on his lap, thrusting his rock-hard cock inside me and making me inhale hard as he filled me up.

Umm, the taste of his mouth.

My head was spinning. His hands squeezed my hips, his yearning indicated by the tension in his grasp. Spencer shifted me against his big dick, its fullness making me feel sensations I'd never experienced.

"Shit, I can feel it," he kept repeating until he quaked, exploding inside his condom.

I expected Spencer to bow out of the shower and leave me alone as if what just happened had never occurred. However, instead of getting up, he gripped the back of my neck, and we made out feverishly. As our tongues dove and slid around each other, I knew I was losing my head and doing something very stupid as far as my heart was concerned.

I could hear my mother chastising me, saying that I should never give a man that much power over me. *He'll break you, Jada. You can't trust him.*

But jeez, Mom, it's only fucking, not marriage.

Then you're doubly wrong, she'd snap back.

I opened my eyes and pulled my mouth off Spencer's.

"What is it?" he asked, dazed.

I leaned back to study the lust in his eyes. Now

he was the one who felt the torture of being abandoned. Oh, what fun it would have been to assume the dominant position for once. But I couldn't. The truth was, he was in control.

"Nothing." I pressed my lips against his again.

Spencer gently gathered my lower lip between his teeth before sliding his tongue down my chin and collarbone until he bit both nipples hard, making me wince. Then I remembered what he'd done to them the other night, which was why they were a little sore. I thought he would give them a repeat performance, but instead he sat me on the bench and parted my thighs.

"Don't move." He trotted out of the shower and quickly returned with a large towel that he folded and put on the wet floor in front of me.

He got on his knees, making firm eye contact. "Baby, I want to see your face while I eat your pussy."

My lips parted, and I took a brisk intake of air as he curled his arms around my slippery thighs and tugged my pussy toward his mouth. I loved his strength. He was a gladiator, a mighty man, the king of my world.

He kept his eyes on my face as his mouth melted over my clit. His tongue brushed along the edge of the sensitive knot, making an instant impact. I cried out then moaned as I made a feeble attempt to cling to the wet bench. The wood offered no support when it came to helping me withstand the escalation of pure pleasure. *Holy shit!* I tossed one arm above my head, trying to hold onto to the wet glass wall, but it was no help either.

The silky sensation of pleasure streaked through my pussy and expanded. I gasped and whimpered, calling for Spencer, who moaned as he kept up the intensity of stroking my clit. Then I screamed at the top of my lungs, pulling in air like a fish out of water as an orgasm possessed my pussy. My thighs trembled, and my body tensed up. The ecstasy consumed me for longer than usual until it eased away, making my body go weak.

I BREATHED HEAVILY WITH SPENCER'S FACE BETWEEN my legs, our hazy gazes connected and his mouth still covering my pussy. I thought he would stop, but Spencer took me there again and again until he brought me down onto the hard floor to absorb my breasts deep into his mouth, biting the tips as he slid my tits in and out of the warm concavity of his mouth. Even the pinch of my nipples between his teeth felt amazing. As I quickened from the ache, he would again sink my perky tits into his moist mouth, soothing them.

"Oh, Spencer," I said. It all hurt—the biting my nipples, the hard floor against my back—but at the same time felt so good.

Then he grabbed a handful of my hair so tightly that I thought he would yank my scalp right off. He twisted my neck, and the pain made me grimace. I was confused by what was happening as I groaned, not knowing whether I should endure so he could eventually get to the pleasurable part or demand that he stop.

Suddenly, Spencer let go of my wet locks, stood up lightning fast, and lifted me to my feet. I was rubbing the back of my neck, looking into his eyes and seeing something I'd never seen before.

"I'm sorry," he whispered. I could tell his throat was tight.

"It's okay…" I chuckled, stretching my neck from side to side. "You just got ahead of yourself."

His serious expression remained unchanged. "I didn't."

I frowned. "You didn't get ahead of yourself?"

He put a hand between us, his palm facing me as if repelling me. "I have to go."

I was still processing that exchange as he walked out the shower so fast I could hardly keep up with my desire to rush after him.

"But, Spencer, it's okay."

He could barely look at me as he snatched a drying towel off the rod. "Finish," he said, pointing at the spout that was still spraying water.

As I watched him dry himself off and put on his pants, I could see that his dick had gotten hard again. He wanted to fuck, and so did I.

"Just come back in and join me," I said, trying not to appear desperate.

He rubbed the towel against his hair, mussing it up. *Damn*, he looked sexy as he tossed the towel on the sink. But he'd dried his hair, sending a message that he wasn't coming back to join me. I stood immobilized, waiting for him to say something, but Spencer didn't even look at me again. He was already walking out of the shower area and was quickly out of sight. I soon felt his absence.

I BROUGHT MY CELLPHONE WITH ME TO THE DINING room. I hated that big, empty, impersonal space. The only thing that kept me from feeling lonely was my memory of making love to Spencer. I could still feel him inside me, his sexy lips on mine, and taste his tongue in my mouth.

I had a fresh-baked toasted baguette with fluffy scrambled eggs, turkey bacon, and homemade shredded hash browns. I ate as if I was famished as I continued reading about the dark Christmases.

The twins, Bryn and Asher, were a hot mess. Asher was the worst of them. He was spoiled but not in the way that he was given everything—he was taught he should have everything simply because of his lineage. He was the sort who shoved square pegs into round holes, grinding the edges until they fit. Of course, the immersion was way too tight and uncomfortable, but he didn't care. He loved convincing himself that he'd gotten what he wanted. He'd persuaded himself that he hated Amelia Christmas because she wouldn't love him. Out of all the Christmas children, Amelia disliked him the most because he reminded her of Randolph.

Bryn, on the other hand, shared more of a friendship-type relationship with Amelia. They weren't best friends but more like two girls who were dorm mates during college and would only be acquainted as long as they lived together. Bryn would start fights in high school and bully other girls just to get her mother's attention. The older brother, Jasper, would sit down with her and ask for insights into why she'd done those things. Randolph Christmas was completely absent in Bryn's life. However, the book talked about encounters she'd had with him during the time her body was blossoming. My jaw dropped as I read about secret hallways and him spying on her nudity. He tried to fondle her, but Jasper had stopped him. It was clear who, at a very young age, was the patriarch of the Christmas family.

"Jada?" Recognizing the voice, I looked up to see Marta standing near the entrance of the dining room.

"Yes?"

"Are you ready for dinner?"

I checked the time in the corner of my screen and jerked my head back. *Shit.* I'd been sitting here for nearly four hours.

"Um…" I dithered, shifting my attention from the screen of my phone to her face. "Can I have dinner in my room?"

She bowed her head, smiling. "Yes, you may."

I rushed upstairs to finish reading about how Jasper Christmas locked horns with his father over putting his hands on Bryn. He'd ventured up to what he called his father's "den of sin," and the man and boy faced off. There was a scuffle. Jasper had made a maneuver and put his father in a head-lock. The account detailed how much Jasper wanted to snap Randolph's neck and put his other family members out of their misery, especially Amelia. Jasper had been amazed by how his father didn't fight back—once he realized his father had been titillated by the tussle, he released Randolph, shoving him away. The old man, who was in his late sixties, hit the leather sofa and stumbled to the floor. Jasper heard something to his right. He quickly turned to see what had made the sound. A tiny girl who couldn't have been a year older than Bryn was trying to remain hidden while peeping out from behind the doorframe. Jasper could see a sliver of her body. The girl was naked, and in her eyes was nothing. No fear, no hope, no grief. She was dead on the inside. His father laughed like a madman. Jasper knew he was drunk and possibly high. But as long as the girl watched both of them, Jasper couldn't look away from her. She wasn't afraid either.

The writer broke away from the story to let Jasper Christmas recount the memory. "I knew I'd seen those eyes before. I couldn't look away from her because I looked into those eyes every day. They belonged to my mother."

I had to put my phone facedown on the mattress as heaviness got stuck in my chest. I pressed a hand over my heart to ease the pressure. It didn't work, and I couldn't stop the tears that filled my eyes either. I could feel his pain as if I were right there with him when he made his discovery. For some reason, I wanted to hug and kiss my mother and father and tell them I loved them. They weren't perfect, but they were far from being on the same playground as Randolph and Amelia Christmas.

I needed a break. The servers had brought dinner a while ago. I wasn't sure when exactly—I'd been too engrossed in the book to pay attention to what was going on around me. Suddenly, an overwhelming desire overcame me. I picked up my phone again, steadied myself, and did what I should have done when I was stranded at the airport. I found my mom's name in my contacts and called her.

Patricia Forte picked up on the second ring. "About time. Where are you?"

Normally, those words would send a pinch of anguish racing through me, perhaps because of the expectations attached to them. "About time" meant I was supposed to have returned all her calls and reported my current life status to her. This time, however, I was still affected by the book and happy to let my mom know every bit of what she wanted to hear.

"Sorry for the delay, Mom. I had to work some stuff out in my life."

"Like losing your job," she said.

I pinched the skin between my eyes. The new-car smell of being accommodating with my mom was fading. "Yes, like losing my job."

"In January?"

I took a deep breath before answering, "Yes, in January."

She went silent, but I could feel her energy chastising me through the phone.

"By the way, how did you find out?" I asked.

"I know how to discover what I need to know," she said in a cool tone that had a threatening edge to it.

"Do you also know where I am now?" I asked, testing just how good her scouts were.

My mom paused, which was a good sign. "Where are you?"

I took a moment to decide whether I should divulge the truth. I had to be careful because if she wanted, she could fuck up my whole situation.

"I'm still looking for a job," I forced myself to say gleefully. However, I wanted to groan. I always felt uncomfortable lying to my mother. "But I have enough in my savings, so you don't have to worry."

"You're lying," she blurted.

My eyes expanded past a comfortable limit. "Huh?"

"You're not in New York anymore. You just had a hefty payment hit your bank account…"

I breathed in sharply as my neck jutted forward. "You have access to my bank account?"

"Your account is twenty years old, darling. I'm the one who set it up for you."

I closed my eyes and shook my head gravely. I hadn't ever thought about changing my bank account. That was something I had to work on pronto.

"But it's my account, Mom, not yours."

"I was worried, Jada. I mean, for all I knew, a

serial killer could have carted you off and left your body decaying in a ditch somewhere while being gnawed on by the billions of rodents who infest that fucking city you refuse to leave."

I sat up straight. My mom had never liked New York City. Her biggest gripe was that she thought the city was grimy. She'd say, "For how expensive it is to live there and visit, you would think they'd do a better job of keeping it clean." Of course, whenever addressing its citizens in a speech, she made them believed she thought it was the greatest city on Earth. I once asked her why she lied so blatantly. I told her she didn't have to bolster their egos—New Yorkers didn't need it.

"Darling, we all need our egos stretched. And my job is not to share with them what I think about their dump of a city—it's to convince them I know they love it." She also didn't like her political colleagues who came from the city. She called them all nutty demagogue wannabes who couldn't reason their way out of a wet paper bag. I didn't agree. Native New Yorkers were more passionate than most. They meant what they said, but we could choose to take their opinions or leave them. Demagoguery wasn't in their DNA—however, survival was. I felt my mom never took the time to learn the difference between the two.

"Jada, are you still there?" my mom asked.

"I'm here." I rolled my eyes, knowing what I had to say next. "Sorry, Mom, I should've told you…"

"Where the fuck are you?" She was done playing nice.

"I'm in Montana," I said, purposely misleading her.

"Montana!" she said as if I'd said I was six feet under and she was speaking to the voice of her former daughter who was haunting her.

"Yes, Mother," I replied, keeping my tone even so she'd know I wasn't rattled by her outburst.

"Are you there alone?"

"No. I'm working, Mom."

"Where are you working?"

I pursed my lips. I could have continued lying and probably should have to avoid another explosion in my ear. "I'm an assistant."

"An assistant?" she bellowed.

My entire body tensed as I jumped to my feet. "Yes, Mom, an assistant."

"Making that kind of money? What the hell are you doing as an assistant?"

I shook my head. "What the hell are you insinuating?" My mind took me back to the shower with Spencer. *He called me "baby." Shit.*

"Jada, why are you pausing?" Mom asked, disturbing my memory.

"You know what, Mom? You kept calling to see if I was alive. I am. Not only am I alive, but I'm a fucking adult who pays her own bills and takes care of herself. I love you, but goodbye."

I didn't even wait for her to finish whatever the hell she was yelling. I ended our call. I didn't have to worry about her calling me back because my device was already programmed to send her calls straight to voicemail. I had to do that, or she would have driven me insane on a daily basis. However, I always carved out time at least twice a month to call her back. I decided to forsake her until I saw her in California for her annual Christmas Eve dinner party. All the gratitude for not being anything like Amelia and Randolph Christmas had faded so quickly into the sea of my anger. I knew that later she would have my dad call to try to smooth things over with us. He was the worst middleman ever, but alas, he dutifully played his role.

After eating some dinner, I became calm enough to continue reading about the Christmases.

The account picked up where it had left off regarding Spencer and Amelia's relationship. My jaw dropped as I ingested the words like a starved animal. I could hardly believe what I was reading.

"What the fuck... shit," I whispered as I reached the end of the chapter.

The shower... the way he'd taken my hair and twisted my neck. It wasn't by accident. Holy shit! *His mother?*

CHAPTER THIRTEEN

JADA FORTE

I t took me a while to fall asleep. I kept hoping Spencer would wake me up in the middle of the night and do me the way he had two nights before. Every inch of me craved his stimulation. He'd opened a portal inside me that only he could walk through. I was unquenchable. I tossed and turned until the wee hours of the morning, trying to find comfort in a bed that normally made me feel as if I was sleeping on clouds.

My alarm clock woke me up. When I turned it off, I saw that a voicemail message from my dad had come through. I also saw that I had eight text messages. They were probably mostly from my mom and a few from Hope.

Hope…

I didn't have enough time to call her, so I texted her that I was still alive and would call her later with an update about Spencer Christmas. I added a winking smiley to give her a clue about what I had to say.

My cellphone dinged when I reached the door. I took it out of my cross-body purse and read the speedy reply from Hope: *Whoa. Wow. Did you do it? Call me as soon as you can.*

I shoved my phone back in my purse, deciding to not respond until we were speaking voice to voice. As soon as I sat down behind my desk, I was off and running. The new week was shaping up to be exactly like the previous one—I would answer as many emails as I could, using the information I had, summarize requests and info for Spencer to address, and attend a mountain of meetings.

Despite being unable to get what I'd read about Spencer and Amelia off my mind, I wasn't so distracted that I couldn't give some attention to the tasks at hand. Spencer had chosen to put some distance between us after getting a little physical with me in the shower. Now that I'd read more about him in the book, I knew why.

My fourth meeting of the day was with Reece Lewis—the head of accounting—and his team. I tried to ignore the fact that one of the women hadn't taken her eyes off me from the moment we'd called our gathering into session nearly an hour earlier. Reese was a fairly handsome guy, but he was one of those people who needed to enrich an environment with his frantic energy. Everything that came out of his mouth sounded like a complaint. Shaking his head, he'd say, "Why are these numbers over here and not there? You can't apply more funds to acquisitions than to maintenance—makes no sense. If Spencer were here, this would be much easier. Where the hell is he?"

That day was no different. Reese said, "I just don't understand how we're going to finalize these numbers before tomorrow's deadline. If he can't come to a meeting like this, how the hell is he going to look over all of the points and approve the dollar amounts?"

It took every ounce of willpower not to roll my eyes or smile condescendingly. Instead, I kept a steady focus on him. "Don't worry about Mr. Christmas. He'll get it done."

Reese's right eye narrowed, and I wondered what he was thinking. Then he stood up lightning fast. "We're done here," he said, frowning as if he was irritated beyond a reasonable level.

After the surprise faded, attendees started leaving the room. I was just about to end the video-conference call when I heard a woman's voice softly say, "Miss Forte."

I froze midmotion and searched the screen for the person who'd said that. I zeroed in on a woman who was a dead ringer for Angelina Jolie, standing close to the camera. She kept checking over her shoulder, making sure everyone kept filing out of the room.

"Yes," I said, keeping my tone official.

The last person had exited, and now the woman folded her arms timidly. "I would like to speak to you in private."

I took my hand off the mouse and sat back in my chair. "Sorry, but I didn't get your name."

"Um…" She raised a finger and went to close the door. "Carol Ludwig." Even though she was alone, she kept her voice low.

I slid my chair closer to my computer screen. "Um, yes. How can I help you, Carol?"

She casually put her face closer to the lens. "He's going to eat you up and spit you out."

I jerked my head back. Her bitter tone took me by surprise, so much so that I questioned whether or not she'd actually said that.

"Sorry?" I asked, feeling my eyebrows constrict.

"He was fucking me, too, so beware. He likes it rough, and then he just disappears," she said as if that had been on her mind for the entire meeting and she'd finally gotten it off her chest.

My mouth had dropped as she turned her back to me. "Wait a minute," I finally said.

She stopped and half-faced me with a cold expression.

My muscles quivered. "First of all, you're out of line. And because of that, I'm going to pretend you never said that."

Her eyes narrowed a pinch. "Then you're not as smart as I thought you were." Without saying another word, she strolled out of the conference room. I sat, immobilized, looking at the empty chairs, wondering what in the hell had just happened.

The knot in my chest felt as if it had grown larger. I wanted a do-over. If I'd had more time to think, I would have said something more centered, like "Mr. Christmas and I maintain a professional relationship, and I ask that you do the same." That would have been more appropriate.

"Shit," I cursed and officially ended the video-conference.

I needed a break to clear my head. I'd been too drawn into the world of Spencer Christmas. I was pretending to be him while working, and I'd readily parted my thighs for him when he appeared in my room. I was reading about him in that damn book, which I wasn't sure I wanted to read anymore. Despite it all, my body, mind, and soul were craving his company. On top of that, I couldn't stop picturing him doing to Carol what he'd done to me.

As I massaged my temples, I imagined saying to Carol, *Thanks for the warning, but I'm not foolish enough to fall head over heels for the likes of Spencer Christmas. Although I am attracted to him. And... my body constantly craves him, which is odd since I can trust him just about as far as I could throw him.*

I sighed sharply and stopped moving. I looked around the room. A familiar chill rushed through me, not because it was cold in the windowless room but because, once again, I had that eerie feel that I was being watched. Thoughts began to mount. I thought about how Spencer had shown up in my room in the middle of the night and about the time he left my room after we first made love. He seemed to be going one way but then stopped himself and went out the door. The book *The Dark Christmases* discussed how the family moved in the shadows of their specially designed mansion.

I got up and walked to touch everything in the office, studying them carefully— the file cabinets, shelves, lamps, fireplace, copier with fax, and Spencer's empty desk. I then stood very still, arms crossed, as my mind tried to convince me to search in a different place. I wondered if Spencer had come into my room through one of those secret passages. Furthermore, where in the hell was his room?

Knowing exactly what to do next, I turned around and ran up the stairs to the main-level. I took the elevator up to the third floor, wringing my hands against my chest the whole way up. I couldn't get to my room fast enough and took off down the hallway as soon as the elevator doors slid open. When I entered my room, I was out of breath.

I stood very still so that I could silence my body and turn up my senses. Slowly, I walked to the top of the staircase. He could have entered through the service elevator that the servers used to set up meals on the lower level of my bedroom, except that when he made that misstep on the first night we made love, his steps were directing him toward the bathroom.

The book said the passageways were always cabinets or standing bookshelves. I dashed to the bathroom area and over to the cabinet that held neatly folded towels and pulled on the side of the structure. It didn't budge. After a brusque sigh, I looked out the window. Then I went into the closet and pulled on the racks for the shoes and all the other constructions.

There was nothing else in this area that could double as the opening to secret hallways. Perhaps the entrance was somewhere downstairs. I snapped my fingers, betting that was it. As I took off, my image in the mirrored walls in the hall that separated the bathroom from the sleeping area made me stop. I studied the glass, and upon completion of my examination, I walked to the edge of the large mirror, dug my fingernails into the space between the back of the mirror and the wall, and pulled gently. To my surprise, it opened.

CHAPTER FOURTEEN

JADA FORTE

I t was as if I'd just stepped into an alternate
universe. The floors were made of concrete,
and so were the walls. It felt like a prison.
The atmosphere was so dark that I had to run back
into the room to retrieve my cellphone. I did it
quickly, fearing that somehow the door would shut
and I'd be locked out.

I turned on the flashlight feature on my cellphone and searched up and down the hollow hall,
trying to get a good sense of direction. I stepped
around in a circle, envisioning where my room was
and how it was situated and pictured myself going
in one direction and then turning the corner. Soon,
my feet followed. Just as I thought, I arrived at a
place that put me behind the staircase that was near

my room. Also, from there I had access to the part of the third floor that was walled off to me in the visible house. I continued down the hall, anxious about the possibility of finding Spencer's room.

All I could hear was the bottom of my shoes carefully walking on the concrete. Every inch of me wanted to turn back and pretend I had never discovered this secret, and that was especially the case when I ran into a dead end.

"Okay," I muttered and headed in the opposite direction. I gave each piece of ground gained special attention. I didn't want to miss anything. I flashed my light beam at the ceiling, the floor, and the walls on both sides of me. Soon, I ran into a flight of stairs that I could actually take. The way heading downward was calling my name, so I went in that direction.

Carefully, I descended the stairs. After the fifth landing with no door leading out of the stairwell, I knew I was no longer in the main house, which only had four levels. I kept my eyes peeled for an exit. I was determined to give up and return to my room when, after one more flight down, I finally reached the bottom. A wide open space led to another concrete-floored, dimly lit hallway.

My heart raced as fear grabbed hold of me. I

still wanted to go back to my room, but my feet carried me forward because I had come so far that there was no use in turning back. But my instincts were on high alert. Finally, I arrived at a white wooden door with a square piece of glass at the top of it. I reached out to turn the knob but then pulled back. What if there were dead bodies in there, and I had to phone the authorities to report what I'd found? I spread the hem of my shirt on the knob, but just as I did that, another cautionary thought entered my mind. What if I needed to prove I'd been there? They would need to find my DNA if they managed to locate this space in the first place.

In the midst of all those grim thoughts, I heard the faint sound of a power tool and felt the vibrations on the bottoms of my feet. The sound came from behind the door, so I hurried up and opened it and padded toward the noise. I cautiously rounded another corner and then stopped in my tracks. I gasped sharply and pressed a hand over my mouth. Way at the end of the hall, illuminated by the light of a floor lamp, was Spencer, dressed in his standard cargo pants and a thick sweatshirt, chiseling away at the wall with something that resembled a jackhammer.

My confused feet didn't know what to do next—

rush in the opposite direction or toward him. Too bad I didn't have a chance to make that decision on my own.

The roaring mixed with the sound of metal pounding cement stopped. I squinted from the bright light stabbing me in the face.

"What the hell are you doing down here?" Spencer roared, his voice bouncing off the wall and socking me in the ears.

"I just…" I realized he couldn't have heard me say that.

His feet pounded the floor, heading in my direction.

Run! the voice in my head yelled.

I decided to obey, turning my back on the light. Before I could take my first step, Spencer's strong hand wrapped around my arm.

"Are you running away from me?" He sounded surprised.

We were face to face, and he was backing me up against the wall. A face mask was pushed back on top of his head, and his skin was sweaty. His eyes looked as if he hadn't slept in days. He looked angry but also a bit intrigued.

I gulped. "Um, sorry for being here. I was just… I mean, I found all of this by mistake."

His eyes narrowed to slits. I was breathing so heavily that I was electrically aware of my chest expanding and deflating.

"This is not the kind of place you find by mistake," he finally said.

I swallowed, knowing exactly what he was insinuating. I knew what the right thing to do was. I had been caught, and perhaps deep down I'd wanted him to see me so that I could tell him what I'd done.

"I read the book," I said.

He shifted his glare away from my face and then back. Spencer scratched behind his ear as he took a step back. My body felt the distance he'd put between us, and so did my heart.

"Get out of here," he muttered.

My jaw slackened and eyes burned. I was at a loss for words. Pressing my lips together, ashamed of myself for being sneaky, I nodded.

"I've asked you not to read the book," he said before I could take my first step.

I shook my head, barely able to look him in the eye. "No, you said you prefer that I not read it."

I didn't think his frown could grow more intense, but it did. Then, striking like a cobra, his lips were on mine and our tongues were swirling around each other, each of us trying to push deeper into the other's mouth. I heard my cellphone hit the concrete as I wrapped my arms around his neck. If only I could merge into his body and we could become one. With each passing second, our kissing turned more passionate.

Suddenly, he ripped his mouth off mine, pressing his forehead onto the top of my head. "Go."

I felt dazed, and his kiss had made me hypersensitive. What I heard him say was *Leave this house—get out of my life*. So I ran like the wind, half expecting him to give chase, draw me back into him, and make mad passionate love to me. But as soon as I had made it to the staircase, I knew for sure that was wishful thinking.

When I made it back to the room, I fell on top of my bed, letting my tears roll freely down my cheeks. I waited for Felix to knock on my door and let me know when a car would be taking me to the airport. The minutes turned to hours.

The ringing of the room phone awakened me. My heart sank as I answered it. "Hello?" I felt heavy and sad.

"Jada, will you be having dinner tonight?" Marta asked.

I sat up quickly. "Does Mr. Christmas…?" I

stopped myself cold when I saw my cellphone sitting on the nightstand. I realized it hadn't been with me when I returned to my room, which meant I'd dropped it in the tunnels. Spencer must have returned it. He had been in my room while I was sleeping again. If he wanted me gone, surely by then he would have directed his staff to ready me for departure.

"Thank you," I finally told Marta. "I'll eat in the dining room."

As I washed my face, which was battered from the crying, I hoped Spencer would find it in himself to join me for dinner.

CHAPTER FIFTEEN

JADA FORTE

The dining room was just as lonely as I remembered it being. I ate alone and hated it the same as I had before. By the time I finished dinner, which was a delicious bowl of shrimp and cheese grits, I knew for sure he would not be joining me. I decided to call Hope to ease my loneliness and put what had happened deep in the catacombs out of my mind. It was three hours later in New York, which made it one in the morning there. However, it was Monday night, and I knew exactly where she'd be.

Hope answered my call on the first ring. "I had just stepped out of the Cantina to call you, my love," she said, sounding extra happy from cocktails and conversation.

"I hear that you're having a ball," I said, trying to not sound sad about it.

She chuckled delightedly, too tipsy to detect my blues. "So, you fucked Spencer Christmas? How was it?"

She said that so loudly that I checked across both my shoulders to make sure no one had heard it. "Keep your voice down," I whispered.

"Oh, shit, Jada. Relax. You're not here. So... how was it?"

I recalled our last kiss, him doing me in the shower, and of course, that first night when he promised to make my first time pleasurable. "It was amazing."

"First of all, you don't sound as if it was that amazing. And secondly, no one's first time is ever amazing. That shit hurts like hell. Unless he has a little dick, but the rumor is, Spencer Christmas is well hung."

After confirming that Spencer was indeed "well hung," I explained to her exactly how he'd done it, using a sex toy and making sure he entered me only when I was climaxing.

"Ah!" Hope screamed so loudly that I jumped. She only did that when she was thoroughly amused. "He should hold seminars on that shit and teach his technique to every fucking dude who takes a stab at virgin pussy! Holy shit, can I rewind the clock and have him fuck me for the first time too?"

I laughed, trying not to picture Spencer doing it with my best friend.

"Uh-oh," she said.

I sat up. "What?"

"You're falling for him. Don't do it."

I felt my eyebrows pull together. "I'm not falling for him." *I think I've already fallen for him.* "We're not going to do it again." There was no need to tell her about what had happened in the catacombs. Plus, that place was a secret, and I was loyal enough to my new boss—and now ex-lover—to keep it that way.

"Okay, but how many times have the two of you had sex?" She sounded as if she was cross-examining me.

I twisted my mouth squeamishly.

"More than once?" she asked.

"Just twice," I said, hoping that was enough to change her mind about me falling for Spencer.

She sighed long and hard. "I'm concerned about you, lovely. You're brand-new at this fucking thing, and sex has a pretty powerful effect on a woman."

I groaned as I rolled my eyes. "You're telling me."

"Right… just remember that it's not real. That's why it's called *making love*—because it could feel like love, but it's really made-up love, not real love that comes from a feeling that's harmoniously produced by the heart and mind."

I swallowed. "Okay, lovely," I said past my tight throat as tears filled my eyes. God, I loved Hope. I knew she was the right person to call at a time such as this. Her steadiness and deep understanding of the human condition made her nonjudgmental, which was why we were best friends.

"Are you sure you can handle the job after boning him?"

"Good question." I visualized the money he'd put in my account. "For now, I can. I'll keep it all business, no more pleasure."

I detected the doubt in her grunt. "Listen, if you slip up and fuck him again, don't beat yourself up about it. Remember, it's not real. What he means to you, how he treats you when his dick isn't in your vag, that's what's real. Understand?"

I groaned, sighed, and closed my eyes to stave off all my intense feelings for Spencer Christmas, which were probably due to our fucking. "I understand."

"Good." She announced that she had to go but would call me soon.

Once we hung up, I was immediately homesick. I should have been at the Cantina that night. I had a feeling I would have been more open to meeting guys and learning about them than I'd been in the past. Men were still such a mystery to me, but being with Spencer Christmas had opened me up to learning more about them.

———

AFTER DINNER, I WENT TO BED. IT TOOK A WHILE to get to sleep. At some point, I had given up hope that Spencer would find his way to my bed. But when my alarm rang, I was still disappointed that it hadn't happened.

When I dressed for the office, I was back to my old habits of making sure I looked good just in case I encountered my boss. I put on a pencil skirt with a tight V-neck sweater that showed off my cleavage. Spencer loved feasting on my tits. If he happened to be spying on me, he would see me in the sweater and race up to the main house to dine on them and on the rest of me.

However, as the day went by in its usual manner, I saw no sign that Spencer Christmas was even in the house. Dillon Gross, one of the investment bankers, complimented me on how nice I looked at the end of our videoconference. He asked me out on a date even though I was in another state.

"Where are you, anyway?" he asked.

The rule was that I wasn't supposed to say. I winked at him. "Far away."

"Then I'll fly you to me, or even better, I'll fly you to wherever you want to go, anywhere in the world, and meet you there."

I smiled at him graciously. His offer was sweet, but I was overly familiar with his type. They chased hard, but after the bait was caught, their love ran weak.

"Thank you very much for the offer, Dillon, but I'm not interested in romantic interludes at the moment. It's not personal."

"Ah… I see," he said, nodding. "He got to you first."

I smashed my lips together harder but then realized the tension in my mouth was giving me away.

"Dillon, I have to go. Have a wonderful rest of your day. I'll have Mr. Christmas look over your proposal."

"Hey." He looked over his shoulder. "He doesn't have to dig deep. It's all in order. We need a signature, and we'll move forward from there."

His flirting suddenly felt like tactical flattery. "I understand," I said.

All the cordiality had drained from his expression, and he looked threatening. "Do you?"

I nodded curtly, keeping it professional. "Of course."

He studied me for a moment and then chuckled. "Are you sure you're not available to join me somewhere?"

"Nope," I said and announced that I had to go.

He reminded me that he needed the forms signed and overnighted to him pronto.

"You'll get them." I ended the call before he could reply.

There was something sleazy about Dillon Gross. I spent a good chunk of time searching for data regarding his special project. I couldn't find anything on any of the databases other than projected returns and a summary of investment destinations, so I spent a lot of time digging deeper.

When that yielded little information, I logged out of my computer as me and logged in as Spencer Christmas and was given access to restricted databases. I was able to locate names of investors attached to Dillon's projects, and the funny thing was that my mother's name and account came up as well as a few other politicos I recognized. At least now I knew why Dillon hadn't wanted me to dig deeper into his project. I suspected he saw my involvement in my mother's investment aspirations as a conflict of interest.

Marta brought me lunch and several snacks as I worked into the early evening. I ate dinner in my room again and made phone calls. First, I talked to my friend Angela, who told me all about how her job sucked, until the recounting of the day's affairs made her stomach queasy and she had to end our call to go throw up. Next, I called Hope and listened attentively as she told me all about the new district attorney, who she said was a cocky and slippery jerk.

"He looks like a mob boss. I bet he's dirty as hell. I wish you were here, because you're really good at assessing people. You'd know, Jada. One conversation with limp dick, and you'd know."

I couldn't help but chuckle. "Okay, what happened between the two of you?"

"Huh?" She sounded surprised.

"What happened?"

Hope sighed in defeat. "Okay, but you can't laugh."

"I won't laugh."

She made me promise again and commenced to tell me about being picked up by a smooth talker the previous night at the Cantina. They had good sex. Lo and behold, she ended up facing him in court that afternoon. He was the prosecutor against her client and used every slimy trick in the book to win.

"But wouldn't he be a defense attorney if he was working for the mob?" I asked.

"Not necessarily," she snapped.

I threw my hands up. "Don't bite my head off. Just beat him at his own game the next time you face him in court, Hope."

Hope went silent. Then she said she would do just that and told me she was tired and had to go. I was tired too.

After I finished eating, I called the kitchen to pick up my dishes and went to bed. I experienced another night of tossing, turning, and hoping

Spencer would wake me up during the night, and again, he didn't.

Another day had arrived. After dressing myself, this time taking less effort to appear attractive for a man who I was sure wasn't going to see, I stood in front of the mirror that opened to Spencer's secret space.

I contemplated not doing it, but after a few minutes, I dug my fingertips behind the frame and pulled. The thing didn't budge, so I pulled harder.

"Ha," I said, scoffing.

Spencer had sealed the entry.

I SAT ON THE EDGE OF MY BED, FEELING SICK TO my stomach. Spencer locking me out of his secrets felt like a kick in the gut and heart. I knew I had no reason to feel upset, but regardless, I did. With a deep intake of air through my nostrils, I closed my eyes. I held the breath, determined to only release it when I was done with Spencer Christmas. It had been two days since I'd seen him. I didn't know whether he was still holed up in the belly of the house or had left the property. *And what in the hell is he looking for in the walls? Gold?*

Bodies? Whatever it was, he didn't want me to know.

I couldn't hold my breath any longer and was forced to let go of it. Spencer Christmas still saturated my heart. The next best thing I could do to banish him from my thoughts was get to work, so I called Marta and asked if my breakfast could be brought to the office, where I went to start my day.

As soon as I was downstairs, I went straight to the inbox. It was empty. In the outbox, on top of Spencer's responses, was a sticky. I snatched off the paper, and my heart turned flips when I read, *Good work. See you soon.*

By noon, Spencer had not fulfilled his promise to see me soon, and that pissed me off. But work kept me from obsessing over him. I was in full throttle. All of Spencer's company managers, directors, and VPs were used to hearing from me. That let me know that I'd made it through the tough part, which was being competent enough to earn their respect. I was also pretty sure being Patricia and John Forte's daughter had something to do with it. No matter how much distance I wanted to put between my parents and me, they always seemed to catch up with me.

By seven o'clock in the evening, I was spent, and I needed to do something new besides going upstairs and calling any of my friends who would engage in a conversation. I decided to drive down to the atrium for a late-day swim.

And as far as Spencer's "See you soon" was concerned, he hadn't shown his face once that day. By the time I shut down my computer and turned off the lights, I had decided to forget that I had ever been attracted to him.

It was freezing cold outside, but I hadn't gotten out of the house in so long that I welcomed it. Sarah looked surprised to see me when I walked in the door. She greeted me with excited hand-waving as I walked in her direction. She had a bag hanging on her shoulder, and she clutched it as if I'd just caught her before she left for the day.

"Heading out?" I asked.

Her smile was unfaltering. "Yep!" She chuckled delightedly. "I guess our meeting was fate. We would keep the doors unlocked, but last month, we found a bear swimming in the pool. It was terrifying and cute. But the water is warm and waiting for you. So how are you enjoying your stay?"

I gave her a hard look. "I'm sorry, but did you say 'bears'?"

"Don't worry, the locked doors have been keeping them out." She pointed to the door. "Your name is programmed into the keypad. Type in 'Jada,' and the door will open for you."

"Oh, thanks."

We smiled at each other for few beats. Then she clutched her bag as though about to leave.

"Oh, and my stay has been quite enjoyable," I said in an effort to keep her around. Now that I knew Spencer's secrets, I understood why he didn't want me to leave the property and why everything around the compound was so hush-hush. I wanted to know if Sarah was part of the vow of secrecy and, if so, figure out how to get her to tell me exactly what Spencer was doing in Wyoming and why he was taking a jackhammer to a wall. "By the way, are you from here?"

Her brows furrowed as she leaned toward me a tinge. "From where?"

"This town."

"Oh." She leaned away again. "I'm from Portland."

"I see. I've been there several times. I love Tuesday Market."

"So do I!" she exclaimed.

I grunted, intrigued, and we stood smiling at each other again. I wondered what she was thinking.

"Well…" she said.

"So do you live on the compound?" I asked before she could wrap up our encounter.

Sarah paused as though deliberating whether to answer my question or not. "I stay in one of the cabins on the north side of the estate."

I intensified my smile. "Are there any bears over there?"

She chuckled. "No… well, yeah. There are no borders around the property. You'd be amazed by the sort of animal traffic we get. It's winter, so a lot of animals are making their way to warmer climates. Just the other day, I saw a herd of buffalo moving across the plains. It was awesome."

"That sounds exciting. I would love to see where you're staying. Maybe we can share a bottle of wine and see what shows up tonight."

Her smile downgraded into a frown. "I don't have wine," she said in a rush.

"Oh," I said, flicking a wrist fluidly. "I can get us as many bottles as we like."

Her gaze wandered. "I don't think Mr. Christmas wants you to…"

"Fuck him," I said, cutting her off.

She quickly turned her back to me. "Sorry, but I can't." She walked away as fast as she could.

I watched her, stunned, and then called, "Sarah."

She stopped and turned to face me.

"The market's on Saturday, not Tuesday. Someone from Portland would've corrected me"—I snapped my fingers—"like that."

She spun on her heels and walked out without saying a word.

I took a swig of wine straight from the bottle and set it back down at the foot of my chair. I hadn't gone swimming. I'd returned to my room and had dinner and wine brought to me. I felt trapped in a world of secrets but knew that all I had to do was call my mom, and she would arrange for a car to pick me up at the gate and take me to her. I dreaded that last part more than being at the ranch. After eating, I sat on the balcony, wrapped in a blanket, and stared out into the darkness. It would snow soon in Wyoming—I could smell it in the air—but I was so hot under the collar that the extra chill in the air didn't cool my skin. I called Hope but got her voicemail. Then I called Rita and Ling, and by some stroke of bad luck, I got their voicemail too. So I wrapped up tighter in the blanket and, as my eyes adjusted to the darkness, used the view of the crystal lake and the mountains in the distance to think about how in the hell I'd gotten to where I was in the first place.

The salary Spencer paid me was still in my account. Other than automatic payments of my credit card bills, none of it had been spent. Just picturing my credit card debt made me groan. When things got tough, I would use them to pay utility bills or buy groceries, and now my minimum payments totaled over two thousand dollars a month.

Debt—that was keeping my ass glued to my seat. My forehead started to freeze, and my nose turned icy. I could feel the cold again, which meant I'd calmed down.

I stood, grabbing my half-consumed bottle of wine off the floor, satisfied with my decision. I would stay, do my job, ask no questions, and stick with the plan of fattening my bank account to pull my finances out of the red and into the black. I stepped into the warmth of my room, slipped the blanket off my shoulders, and went to bed, knowing Spencer Christmas would not be joining me.

***

WHEN I WOKE THE NEXT MORNING, I REMEMBERED the vow I'd made before going to bed. But as I walked down to the office, Felix was opening the front door for someone. My heart sank when I saw who it was.

CHAPTER SIXTEEN

SPENCER CHRISTMAS

I sat across from Mita, barely able to keep my eyes open. The slight crinkling of her forehead told me that she was trying to keep a straight face.

"When was the last time you slept?" she asked.

She had a way of making concern sound clinical. I liked that about her. I didn't want her pity. I didn't want anyone's pity.

I shrugged. "It doesn't matter."

"Is there a reason you haven't been able to sleep?"

My head was aching like crazy. I massaged my temples vigorously, trying to get some relief. "Because I'm close. That's why." I didn't know what the hell I'd just said. Whatever it was felt reckless.

"Are you ready to tell me what you're hoping to discover?"

I let my palms slap down on the leather sofa and sighed deeply. I probably should have cancelled our session, but I wanted to talk to Mita, not about my search but about Jada. "I just need some fucking answers."

She kept a steady and strong posture. "Answers about what?"

"Jada," I blurted.

She nodded softly. "I see." She finally took out her notepad and started flipping the pages. "Last week you mentioned you were fascinated by your new employee. Has that evolved?"

Oh, has it ever. No matter what I did, I could still smell Jada Forte's skin and feel my cock inside her warm, wet pussy. But I wasn't going to tell my therapist that.

I shrugged. "Some."

"Please elaborate," she said in that even tone of hers.

"Well…" I shifted in my seat. "I crossed the line with her."

"You had sexual relations?"

"Yes, but more than that."

She nodded, letting me know that she was listening.

"I almost hurt her while fucking, but I stopped myself."

"You stopped yourself. That's good," she said as if that were some minor victory.

I shook my head. I didn't think she understood what was really happening to me. Hell, I couldn't comprehend it. Jada Forte was probably the sexiest woman I'd ever fucked. She had a real sensuality about her, a hidden one that not even she could see. And *damn*, did that turn me on. I wanted to consume her, carry her with me every minute of the day, fuck her, look at her, talk to her—I could never get enough of her, and that scared the hell out of me.

"Do you have any words for the thoughts you're having?" Mita asked.

I sat up straight. There was something about the way she asked that question. I knew I'd better say something. "I don't know why I feel this way about her. I've been with a lot of women, but she…"

"But," she said, flipping through her notepad, "you said that you've never been able to feel complete sexual arousal during sex." Now she was reading whatever the hell she'd written verbatim. "You've never been able to feel an orgasm, and the sensations leading to an orgasm felt numb." She looked up, watching me, waiting for a response to her description of a situation that used to make me feel like less of a man.

I nodded.

"But the numbing wasn't present when you were with this woman sexually?"

Memories made my dick throb, and I felt embarrassed because I was alone with the wrong woman. "Yes," I said curtly.

"And is that why you haven't been able to sleep?"

I swallowed that big fat lump. "It's not the only reason. I'm almost done here. I haven't found what was I looking for. But I hired this woman, and she's..." I took deep breath and squeezed my eyes shut. "I just didn't see her coming."

When I opened my eyes again, Mita was watching me with calm. "Whatever you're looking for here, when you find it, what are you hoping your discovery will do for you?"

I looked off, grimacing at the fucking carpet. "I've tried to answer your question many times before." I scratched the back of my head.

She shifted abruptly. "Then let me ask you another question. Are you afraid that Jada Forte will have an adverse reaction to whatever you find?"

I closed my eyes as I felt a hard lump in my chest. It was about genes. I was my father's son. Every woman should stay clear of me.

"I've done some fucked-up shit in my lifetime, Mita. Shit that Jada could never perceive."

She scooted to the edge of her seat. "Use your tools. Take a moment to deconstruct what you just said to me, look at it differently, and rephrase it."

I did what she instructed and then opened my eyes. It was if the doctor's face was aglow with wisdom.

"The past was what it was. I can let it drag me under and define me by shit I didn't know how to change, or I can change because of what I know now."

She showed me her big beautiful smile and sat back in her chair. "Yes, Spencer. You are who you are, sitting right in front me. That's the real you—the man who can now allow himself to feel pleasure without pain. But here's the thing about love—you don't get to control whether or not the other person loves you. Be yourself, the man sitting in front of me, having your past, present, and future, and she'll get to decide if she wants to love you. Or is that the part that scares you? She's falling in love with you, and you're afraid of it?"

Her words made me incline backward. *Love?* Never had I thought I would feel that. I loved my siblings when they weren't being assholes. We all had our shit. Jasper had come a long way since Holly. He said it was because he loved her and she was good for him. I never thought I would find someone I could feel the same way about. *Is Jada my Holly?* I didn't know. I didn't have to have an answer at that very moment, but I had to come up with one soon.

"Maybe," I finally replied.

The alarm rang, ending the day's session.

WHEN I WALKED MITA TO THE DOOR, I WAS HOPING to find Jada lurking. I could tell she was a little jealous of my therapist, which turned me on. Mita got into the car and drove off, and my dick got hard as I thought about letting myself make love to Jada without letting mental barriers get in the way. *Shit.* The excitement was stirring in my dick. I wanted her. I wanted her badly. But I would have to wait for the right moment.

I had work to do, and so did she. But later…

I will find her.

I will fuck her.

I will enjoy it.

CHAPTER SEVENTEEN

JADA FORTE

That day, the mysterious woman had worn a black-and-white plaid suit that hugged her flawless curves. I couldn't get the sight of her walking into the foyer out of my head. I covered my face with my hands, kicking myself for not smiling back at her. Instead, I'd turned away from her and practically run to the office.

I forced myself to get through the day, sitting in on more meetings and taking notes for Spencer. I couldn't face Sarah after our awkward conversation of the previous day, but I needed to get out and away. I couldn't stand to be cooped up in the windowless office or go to my room. It was time to clear my head. So I shut down my computer and headed out of the office. I took the elevator to my room to grab a coat and then rode back to the main floor and headed out of the house quickly enough not to catch Felix's attention. I didn't want him asking me where I was going or what time I'd be back for dinner. The truth was, I didn't know.

The golf cart was waiting in front of the house, as always. I climbed in behind the wheel and turned up the heat before driving off. A rebel's spirit gripped me as I drove past the atrium and went as far as my courage would take me. Instead of focusing on the worry that Spencer had eyes everywhere and at some point, one of his rule enforcers would probably stop me, I decided to focus on the shimmering lakes on both sides of the road, which were surrounded by wild grass or splays of trees. It was as if every mile presented a new and beautifully lush landscape. The farther away from the ranch I drove, the more the trees thickened the land and disrupted the view of the mountains. I figured at some point I would run into the cabins Sarah had mentioned. My heart was beating like crazy. I was probably going way too far away from home. The more ground I gained, the more anxiety rattled on my insides.

Suddenly, I heard droplets pelting the top of the cart and then ice hitting the window.

"Shit," I muttered. I'd known the snow was coming, but I didn't think it would arrive so soon.

The trees kept getting thicker, and the road turned powdery white. I didn't want to call my excursion a bust, but it was time to turn around and head back to the ranch. I pressed the brake, eager to make the three-point turn and drive out of thick brush. As I turned the wheel, the sounds of growling, barking, and something like a cow mooing filled the cab.

"What the hell?" I muttered, checking my driver-side mirror. I tried to look in the one on the passenger side, but ice had collected on the glass, and I couldn't see through it.

The wild noises got louder, closer. I sat very still. Then I felt the impact and heard it too. My tiny cart spun in circles, and I felt as if I were trapped in a screaming, howling, bumpy vortex.

"Shit!" I screamed as I got hit again.

My heart wanted to jump out of my chest, and my instincts warned me that now was not the time to lose control of the situation. Whatever was happening to me, I was in trouble.

Boom, thump, clunk! I heard a deep, guttural whine. Something was hurt, angry, and ravenous. I was still spinning and directing my wheel toward the movement of the tires. When I was at Redmond College, I'd driven all the way across the country to California for the holiday months, to my parents' chagrin, and my dad had given me a long lecture about the maneuvers to pull if I found myself in different car-accident scenarios. I was experiencing one of those options at the moment.

Finally, the cart came to a stop. My eyes expanded as I looked at what was going on beyond the windshield. I could hardly believe what I was seeing. A pack of gray-and-white wolves were tugging at a small animal that resembled a moose, and larger moose—perhaps the mother—was trying to heave her antlers at them.

I wanted to get the hell out of there as fast as I could, but I would have had to drive off the road to get around the spectacle. I squeezed the sides of my face, panicking. I screamed along with the mother moose as one of the wolves pulled at the baby moose's leg.

I grew dizzy and thought I would pass out. Never in my life had I seen such a thing. Then my cart shook again as the mother moose started kicking it, perhaps taking her anger out on me. I was shaking again, hoping my cart didn't get turned over. The wolves were still trying to bring the smaller moose down, but it fought vigorously for its life.

"The horn," I said, searching frantically. My hands and body were so shaky that I wouldn't have been able to find if it was on the tip of my nose.

As I scrambled around, trying to find the horn, I heard two loud cracks that sounded like gunshots. The wolves howled and rushed away from their dinner. To my surprise, as soon as they were gone, the baby moose tried to stand. The mother moose went over to help it, bellowing as if in severe emotional pain.

I stared into the bright headlights of a big truck facing in my direction. I wanted to get out and run to whoever was driving it, but I was too afraid to pass the mama moose still crying over her baby, who might never recover from the assault.

"Drive around them now," a projected voice said. There was no doubt who it was—Spencer Christmas.

Slowly, I began to drive, creeping past the mama moose. At first, I was thankful to be saved. Then remorse gripped me because I shouldn't have been way out there in the first place. I stopped the car beside his truck and couldn't stop shaking as Spencer carefully approached my door, aiming what appeared to be a shotgun at the mother moose. Now I felt even worse than before. It was probably because of me that her baby had gotten caught by the wolves, and if she attacked me again, Spencer was sure to end her.

When he made it to my door, I had to unlock it. I didn't even remember locking it. He put his finger over his lips as he opened it. The golf cart must have been masterfully soundproof because as soon as the outside was let in, I could really hear the mother moose wailing.

He took me by the hand. "Let's go," he whispered.

I pulled back a little. "What about the baby?"

"Now," he demanded, ignoring my plea to help the baby moose.

I was certainly not going to fight him on this. The mother moose was a fierce creature indeed. In no time, I was out of the cart and keeping pace with Spencer, who led me to the passenger side of one of the biggest trucks on the planet. I climbed the steps that led to the front seat and got in.

He closed the door behind me. The wolves were back, and the mother moose was bucking them again but was losing the fight. When Spencer finally plopped himself behind the steering wheel, the wolves, not at all concerned about the big moose, were watching the truck while dragging their dinner into the trees. The mama moose looked on as if stunned by what had just happened.

"We can't do anything?" I asked, feeling the strain on my face and in my body.

"That's what happens in the wild, Jada. What the fuck are you doing all the way out here, anyway?" His voice echoed so loudly in the cab that I had to duck a little to bear it.

"I know I fucked up, Spencer. And what are you doing here? How did you find me?"

He leaned back and pressed his lips together as if not prepared to answer my question. "Why do you keep doing what I ask you not to do?"

The cat had my tongue. There was no way I could tell him I was searching for secrets I thought he might be keeping. "I just wanted to go exploring, that's all."

"You can't go exploring on this property, especially without a guide!" There was no doubt he was angry as he shoved both hands toward the windshield. "And now do you see why? I don't have a fence around the borders."

I wondered why not, but I sure wasn't going to ask while we were in this emotional state. Plus, I was still shaken up after witnessing the cold viciousness of nature. Spencer seemed way too unfazed by it. The mother moose was still looking into the dense woods. She watched us as Spencer made the perfect three-point turn. I wanted to turn around and see what she'd do next, but I felt a heavy sense of guilt for disobeying Spencer's rules.

"I apologize," I finally said, keeping my eyes on the snow being pushed aside by the windshield wipers.

He didn't say anything, so I turned to look at him. Spencer appeared confused by my apology as he kept shifting his attention between the road and me.

"I only want you to be safe," he finally said.

I kept my focus out the window and away from him. I'd already apologized to him, so there was nothing else to say. I only had questions I knew he wouldn't answer, like how in the hell he'd known I was in a pinch. The snow was sprinting to the earth, but I tried to see if I could find a tiny red light attached to the branches. There had to be a surveillance system somewhere out there. Then I was struck by a realization—it was the golf cart. It must have had a tracking device on it.

"I also apologize," he said.

I frowned, confused. "Apologize for what?"

"My tone. I've been working on softening it for a while. Mostly I fail, but sometimes I don't."

I cocked my head. "Hmm… no. You've only failed."

Spencer snorted. "As I said, I'm working on it. But what happened to you today is a rarity. If you want to go horseback riding or see more of the property, just ask."

"Ask who?" I replied bitingly. "Because you're never around, and I…" I slumped in my seat, feeling deflated. "I just wish you'd start telling me the truth. Because then I'd know you care."

It felt as if time had stopped. I was proud of myself for being emotionally honest with Spencer. We had a lot to discuss if he wanted us to keep having sex. Now that I'd had sexual intercourse a few times, I realized I wasn't one of those people who could fuck simply for enjoyment. I wasn't built that way. I loved the connection part of sex, not merely his dick being inside me and my pussy bursting with orgasms. I wanted it all—his heart and the pleasure.

Spencer stopped the truck in front of the steps and turned to me. His features were smooth, expressionless. We stared at each other for a long time.

"I want you to go to your room," he whispered slowly.

My mouth was caught open, and I couldn't think of a response as I watched him hop out of the truck as if the distance to the ground was no problem and trot around the front. As soon as he opened my door, the stepladder folded down. Spencer didn't look at me once as he turned his back on me and went into the house.

CHAPTER EIGHTEEN

JADA FORTE

When I made it to my room, I stripped out of my damp pants. The crotch of my panties was wet too. "Shit," I cursed under my breath.

That was not a good sign. My desire was at odds with my mind. I didn't want Spencer Christmas to excite me merely by being in my presence.

I took off my shirt and shuffled to the closet to drop them in the laundry basket, determined to learn how to contain myself around him in the future. Before I could reach my desired space, two strong arms wrapped me up from behind. I gasped when a large, hard bulge drove into the crease of my ass.

"I've missed you," Spencer whispered in my ear, his warm breath filling the canal.

My body went into erotic shock. He kept grinding my ass, pinching my nipples through my bra, and sucking on the side of my neck. The air I took in filled my throat. He guided me around to face him, and all my vows of self-control went out the window as his lips seized mine and his tongue followed. My head spun as Spencer led me. He could have taken me anywhere, but I knew we were going to my bed, and then my back was pressed against the mattress.

Spencer's hooded gaze was ravenous with lust as his body abandoned mine and he stood at the side of the bed, watching me. I wanted to twist and turn with desirous need, but instead, I was held captive by the way he watched me.

"I want you to trust me," he said.

I nodded and shifted to sit up.

He put his palm gently on my chest and pressed me back down onto the bed. "Don't get up."

My body felt heavy as I contemplated whether to go along with whatever was happening. Spencer continued watching me with a burning lust in his eyes.

"I want you so bad," he whispered. His

manhood, pressing against the material of his loose-fitting sweatpants, told the same story. His Adam's apple bobbed as he swallowed and then grunted to clear his throat. "You want the truth?"

I frowned. This was strange indeed. I wondered whether we were about to have sex or a conversation.

"You read the book."

I propped myself up on my elbows. "Yes," I said tentatively. "But are we really going to talk about that now?"

"We have to, baby, because all the shit you read about me was true. It's why I've been fucked up when it comes to women and relationships.

He will eat you up and spit you out. Carol's words haunted me. Then everything I'd read about him and Amelia Christmas came back to mind.

"Is it because of what your mother…?"

"She wasn't my mother," he retorted.

I squeezed my eyes shut, remembering that tidbit. "Sorry. I meant Amelia."

"Partly." He smashed his lips together thoughtfully. "Some of it. But I'm freed from that shit. This thing we have together is new to me. I want it to work, but I don't know what you want. Or how you want it."

"Do you mean in terms of sex?"

He nodded and shrugged gently, and I saw a vulnerability he'd never expressed before.

A smile formed slowly on my lips. "You've been doing it just fine so far."

Spencer cracked a smirk. "That's good to know."

I sat up quickly and reached out for his hand. His lascivious gaze slid from my face—stopping at my tits, his eyes narrowing slightly—then slipped down to my hips and back to my face before he took me up on my offer. He straddled me and parted my thighs to lie between my legs.

"Shit," he whispered, kissing and sucking on my neck, which sent shivers down to my pussy. "I shouldn't have done this."

His nearness and lips and tongue on my neck made my head spin.

"Done what?" I whispered.

Spencer rolled onto his back and slid a condom out of his pocket. "Take these off," he said, tugging at the band of my panties. He pointed his head at my bra. "And that."

I yanked my crotch-soaked panties down my legs and tossed them somewhere in the room. Then I unclipped my bra, tugged it off, and flung it too.

Anticipation made me gulp—I couldn't take my eyes off the sheer size of his engorged cock. When the condom was on, he rolled on top of me again, lying between my separated thighs, and drove his erection deep into my inner sanctum. I sighed, holding on to him tightly.

His skin was warm, his muscles hard in skin supple. He kept repeating how soft I was, how wet and warm. We clung to each other like crazy. *Deep* wasn't deep enough with each stroke of his dick inside my pussy. We only broke lip contact to express indulgent pleasure with sighing, moaning, or grunting.

"I can feel you," he kept repeating.

"I can feel you too," I whispered.

The shift was rapid. Spencer rotated from on top of me, and the next thing I knew, my ass was at the edge of the bed and Spencer's face was between my legs, arms wrapped around my thighs and his hot mouth and soft tongue stimulating my clit.

I moaned, squirming against his face as pleasure raced through my pussy. And then the erotic sensation diminished. Breathing heavily to slow down my excitement, I opened my eyes to see what had happened. Spencer's mouth had abandoned my mound, and he was watching me.

"What is it?" I asked breathlessly.

He immediately went back to pleasuring me with his mouth, the impact forcing my palms down on top of the bed. I dug my fingernails into the sheets. He had a vise grip on my lower half as the electricity of a slow-building orgasm swelled in my pussy.

"Umm…" he moaned as if I tasted like the best thing since cherry pie.

"Oh, Spencer," I said airily and cried out as an orgasm swirled like a whirlwind through my pussy. Before my lower body had stopped pulsating, my legs were spread wider, Spencer's bare chest was on mine, and my pussy was filled with his rock-solid cock. I held him tightly as he pounded the hell out of me. His thick shaft, agitating my most sensitive parts with every rapid thrust, made me feel unbelievable pleasure. I could hardly stand it as my eyes widened and I took in a hard breath, guiding my hips toward the same sensation that had ignited my pussy when Spencer went down on me.

I kept calling out to the Almighty as what I felt got stronger and stronger. Then pleasure erupted through my mound, and Spencer cursed the air as he, too, exploded with orgasm.

WE WERE IN BED, AND I WAS LYING AGAINST Spencer, who had his arms wrapped around me. My pussy felt perfectly comfortable as he had cleaned it gently with a warm towel and then kissed me tenderly. Fastened securely in his embrace, I thought my heart would burst from something that felt a lot like love.

"About the book…" He drew me in closer.

The heaviness left my eyelids. "I know. You didn't want me to read it."

"That's not why I brought it up." He lifted my hair off my neck and kissed my skin. "I want you to listen to me carefully."

"Sure," I said, ready to hear anything he had to say.

He fell silent for moment. "The book is wrong."

My breath hitched. "How so?"

"I've always known about Amelia. You and Mita are the only ones I've told this."

My eyebrows furrowed. "Mita?"

"Mita Sharma, my therapist. You've met her twice."

My jaw dropped as I rotated to look him in the face. "The beautiful woman is your therapist."

He smiled faintly. "You're beautiful too." He kissed my lips and then went on to tell me more about his past.

Amelia Christmas had told Spencer he wasn't her son when he was thirteen years old. She'd noticed Randolph trying to make Spencer into a carbon copy of himself and decided he needed to know the truth to save his soul, so one day, she sat him down and told him everything about herself.

But Amelia made him promise not to ever say a word to anyone. "You understand how dangerous your father is, don't you?"

When she said his father was dangerous, it made perfect sense to Spencer, who'd known about the prostitutes and the young girls. He wouldn't get into the specifics with me, but he said Randolph Christmas was the kind of man who did whatever was needed to get exactly what he wanted.

"About sex…" He gulped nervously. "I never liked it. When I did it, I couldn't wait for it to be over. When I came, my dick couldn't feel it because of the fucking shame." He drew me closer. "I haven't felt anything until you."

I wanted to weep with joy. I didn't know if he could handle what I was thinking, but I said it anyway. "Then we were both virgins."

He chuckled. *Gosh*, I loved the sound. Then we fell silent again. Our one light moment didn't mean the story was over.

"What about the other part?" I asked. "The rough sex."

His grip on me loosened, but he didn't let go. He said that part of the book was true, but he knew he wasn't involved with his mother, even though he spent most of his life wanting her to love him as a mother should. Back then, he loved to fight and often went out in search of a brawl. The first week after he graduated from college and came home, he got into a fight in a bar in Providence. Normally, the cops would look at his license, see his name, and let him go, but the one who arrested him that time hadn't gotten the memo. He called Amelia, and she came down to the station to get him. On the way home, she pulled the car over and taunted him, trying to get him to hit her by calling him every name in the book—"pussy," "bastard," "loser." But when she called him the reject of a dead mother who was a crack whore and piece of trash, he socked her so hard that she spat blood. Amelia chuckled, showed him her bloody teeth, and repeated what she'd said. She told him to hit her again, and he did. Then she practically ripped his pants open. He was surprised at how fast he'd gotten hard. Then she did something to him that shocked the hell out of him. When he came, he still felt numb, but it was the closest he'd ever come to feeling something during sex.

They engaged in the same sort of antics for about a week. Then Amelia didn't want to do it anymore and went back to pretending he didn't exist. He turned to a prostitute who his father had rejected because she'd gotten too old, and she'd agreed to oblige him with the kind of sex Amelia had gotten him used to having.

"And that's the whole sick and twisted story." He chuckled nervously. "And that's also why I have a fucking shrink."

The silence blared loudly, and I knew he was waiting for my response. But my tears had been rolling since the beginning of the recounting of his life story as I thought about the pain the young Spencer must have felt. I sniffed and wiped the tears from my cheeks.

"Are you crying, baby?" He turned me around to see my face. I didn't hide my feelings as I looked him in the eye.

My stomach fluttered, and my heart swelled. *Don't say it, Jada.* I didn't have to. Spencer guided himself on top of me, and I spread my thighs. The tip of his manhood stretched the entrance of my pussy until his shaft pushed through my wet and willing walls. We held on tight to each other as we brought into existence what my heart felt and made love.

———

WE'D DONE IT AGAIN AND AGAIN AND THEN FALLEN asleep. When I opened my eyes, my greatest hope had been actualized: Spencer hadn't gone anywhere. Then I remembered that I had to get to the office, and I sat up with a gasp.

He sat up too. "What is it?"

I flung my legs over the side of the bed. "I have meetings today."

Spencer curled an arm around my waist and guided me to lie back down. He positioned himself between my legs. "Don't worry about work."

"But you hired me to…" I gasped as he stuffed his erection inside me.

"The boss says you stay right here," he whispered, pumping his thickness in and out of my pulsing wet walls.

As the hours passed, our sexual encounters had

taken several approaches. We'd straight-out fucked, me on my knees and Spencer pounding my pussy from behind. We'd engaged in gymnastics, my legs way up here and his way over there, contorting our bodies into this position and that position.

We were making love again, our gazes intimate this time, seeing behind the eyes. I had no doubt Spencer felt the same way about me that I did about him. The fact that it had happened so soon after we met scared the hell out of me, but I trusted him. The jury was still out about whether that was a good or a bad thing.

After I climaxed and he did the same, Spencer wrapped me in his arms. The sun had fallen, and the glow from the lamp on the nightstand radiated sensually throughout the bedroom.

I sighed gently. "What next?"

He was silent for a long time and then said, "What are you referring to?"

"Work. You're my boss, and you're paying me a hell of a lot of money." I chuckled. "Hope and I joked about sex being part of my job duties since the salary was so high."

Spencer moaned. "I like the sound of that."

I nudged him playfully with my elbow. He snorted and kissed the back of my shoulder.

"Seriously, Spencer, we've fucked ourselves into a precarious situation here."

"I don't see it that way."

I pressed my lips together. Maybe I was over-thinking it. I did that a lot, which was why I'd been a virgin for so long. "My assignment here is over in six months."

"I don't want you to go in six months. You've done a fine job, Jada. Even if I don't use you in the same capacity, I'd like for you to stick around, same pay—including the fucking."

I chuckled. "What about Carol?" I asked and instantly wanted to take it back. We hadn't discussed her warning.

"Who's Carol?"

"Carol Ludwig."

"I don't know who that is. And why are you asking me about her?"

I turned to look at him incredulously. "She works for you. She's part of Reece Lewis's team in accounting."

"Okay, but what about her?"

"She warned me about you. Said you would fuck me and then leave me like you did her."

He shook his head. "I don't remember her. I would have to see her. My problems with sex never stopped me from trying to fuck as many women as I could." He took a deep breath. "I don't remember this Carol Ludwig, but I'm sorry that she feels that way. I have a lot of amends to make, and the fact that I fucked one of my employees and she's upset enough to warn you about me troubles me."

I swept my hand softly down the side of his face. "Gosh, where did you come from, Spencer Christmas?"

He seized my wrist and trailed kisses down my arm. Then his tongued lapped my nipple several times until he raked his teeth across the tip. I gasped as he flipped me onto my back. Spencer licked, kissed, and nibbled his way down my sternum until his wet, warm tongue slid up my slit, and his mouth latched onto my clit.

Knock, knock, knock.

I stopped moaning and looked toward the door. Spencer's pleasure-bringing tongue never let up, and he even slipped fingers inside me, finger-fucking fast and deep.

"Ah," I said, breathing heavily while tipping my hips toward his stimulation.

Knock, knock, knock.

The electric sensation of a burgeoning orgasm

went away. When I opened my eyes, Spencer's face was moving toward mine.

"Tell them to wait," he said.

I nodded rapidly. It took all my self-control to steady myself enough to call, "Wait a minute."

He winked. "Good job."

"You're not done yet, big brother?" a woman said from behind the door.

Spencer jerked his head back. "Bryn!"

The door opened, and a beautiful woman was standing there. She had fine blond hair with beach waves and wore a long skirt with a kaleidoscope pattern and blousy tube top that showed off her toned midriff. She smirked and leaned against the doorjamb.

"Hi, Jada Forte. I'm Bryn," she said, grinning at me.

CHAPTER NINETEEN

JADA FORTE

T*alk about not understanding boundaries!*
Bronwyn Christmas had no concept of them, which was exactly how she'd been portrayed in the book. She stood in the doorway while her brother was still between my legs.

"Get the hell out of here!" he shouted. "And close the door."

"Oh, come on, Spence. It's me."

"Out!" he shouted.

She hadn't budged an inch. "I've seen you do this before, although you seem"—she rolled her hand—"more comfortable with it somehow."

Her words gave him a sort of super strength,

and he seemed to float backward off the bed and stand.

"Please leave," I said before Spencer could say anything else.

Bryn cocked her head, watching me curiously. But Spencer was approaching her quickly. She took a step back, away from the doorjamb, and he slammed the door and locked it.

Spencer then went into the bathroom, wet a towel with warm water, and wiped my pussy as he normally did.

"Did you know she was coming?" I asked.

"No," he snapped.

By the wrinkling of his eyebrows, I knew he didn't want to talk about it anymore. The last thing he said before putting on his dark-blue loose-fitting sweatpants was, "I planned to fuck you all night long." Then he walked to the door, telling me to join them for dinner in half an hour, and left my room.

I had no idea how he did it, but I wanted to follow Spencer Christmas's every order. I also wanted to look pretty before arriving to the table. However, Carol's warning remained stuck in my mind as I studied myself in the mirror. She was a sexy woman—sort of a vixen. I was... I blinked at the image staring back at me. I was certainly pretty. I'd been told that my whole life. Lots of men called me hot, but I never accepted that definition or considered it a compliment. Dogs were in heat, not people and certainly not me. It was my mom who'd taught me to see compliments that way. She had a lot to do with how I perceived myself.

"Jada, in this world you'll have beauty capital, but only a weak woman relies on that to get whatever the hell she wants." She would take me by the chin and look me in the eye. "Your father and I gave you a beautiful face, but we also blessed you with intellect, killer instincts, and self-control. Remember that."

I had no doubt my mom was the reason I'd been a virgin for most of my twenties, and that wasn't a bad thing, especially considering how pleasurable my first time was. Everything about that first night with Spencer was right. The stars had aligned. We were both exactly where we needed to be in life to make our connection that much stronger.

"So fuck Carol," I said to the image in the mirror. And by the way my reflection looked at me, she agreed.

Spencer wouldn't just leave me. He wasn't the

same man for me that he'd been to her. And I no longer cared what Spencer was hiding, though I was sure that he was hiding something—not just from me but from everybody, including the towns-people, which was why everyone I encountered was from out of town.

I had on my tight black, mid-length skirt with a matching deep V-neck camisole that showed just how naturally fantastic my tits were. That was something else I could thank my mother for. I'd fortunately packed party clothes in the mistaken belief that there would be a place in Jackson Hole where I could go out and do some socializing.

I gave myself one more long study in the mirror. I barely recognized the woman staring back at me.

My nerves were tightening and twisting into knots as I walked down to the dining room. Spencer's sister was what I considered a radical element. She seemed unpredictable and unable to respect boundaries. After the last two days of making love to Spencer more times than I could have dreamed of, I felt as if her showing up unannounced had thrust me into a whole new aspect of being with Spencer that I wasn't ready for.

As I walked down the stairs, I wondered what we were to each other. Boyfriend and girlfriend? Boss and employee? Fuck buddies? Friends? All the above? I hoped Bryn wasn't cruel enough to put us in the position to have to verbally define our relationship.

"Good evening, Miss Forte," Felix said once I'd made it to the bottom of the stairs.

I jumped, startled, and turned toward him. "Good evening, Felix."

I heard voices and turned in that direction. Spencer said something, and even though I couldn't make out the words, his tone indicated that he wasn't happy. Then Bryn spoke. She sounded lively.

I sighed and rolled my eyes. She was purposely pushing his buttons—that was for sure. I recalled the emails she'd sent Spencer. In them, she sounded contrite and evolved, nothing like the rabid little witch who would barge in on her brother while he was having sex.

"Are you ready to be escorted to dinner, Miss Forte?" Felix said.

I whipped my attention back to him. "Um, no, thank you, Felix. I'll just follow the noise."

He bowed. "As you wish."

I watched Felix walk off to wherever he spent most of his waking hours. That was still a mystery. Spencer was speaking again and sounded just as annoyed as he'd been before.

There was no more time to delay. I stepped off toward the dining room, chin up, back straight. It was time to face the sister from hell.

"Good evening," I said as I entered the dining room.

Spencer, who was sitting at the head of the table, stood. Bryn watched him with wide, amused eyes and a wicked smirk.

"You look beautiful tonight," he said, still gazing at me as if I were all lit up.

My head felt as if it was detached from my neck as I stood, captured by his insistent gaze.

"Wow, the first and only woman who's ever caught the slipperiest fish in the ocean," Bryn said.

Only then did he release me from his intent stare to frown at her. "All right, Bryn. We have company. Give it a break."

She scoffed. "How soon we forget how you always treated my guests."

Spencer pointed to the place setting to his left, across the table from where Bryn was sitting. "Jada, sit here." His cold, controlling tone and deep frown were back with a vengeance.

"Sure." I walked happily to my seat and made myself comfortable. My goal was to inject a different sort of energy into the air.

Bryn studied my every move with that amused look in her eyes. "So, Jada…" Her mouth remained stuck open as Spencer reached out for my hand. I relished the contact of our skin as our fingers entwined. Never in a million years would I ever get enough of Spencer Christmas.

"Yes, Bronwyn?" I said, my attention still mostly on Spencer.

She grunted, intrigued. "My brother seems to think people can't change. However, it appears that doesn't apply to him."

"That's not what I'm insinuating." Spencer released my hand to shake both of his in front of his face. "Now you're a fucking hippie? Get out of here, Bryn. I don't buy your peace, love, and niceness. What the hell do you want? Why the hell are you here?"

She rolled her eyes and sighed deeply. "I'm a work in progress, big brother. I know I behaved like a fucking cunt earlier. I shouldn't have walked in on you and Jada,"—she nodded at me—"while you were, to my pleasant surprise, actually enjoying yourself. I mean, good for you."

"Fuck you, Bryn," he spat.

She threw her hands up as she sighed. "That was a fucking compliment, Spence. Jeez, I can't win for losing." Then she set her attention on me. "Wasn't that a compliment, Jada? Oh, and only assholes who I no longer associate with call me Bronwyn. Call me Bryn."

"Well, Bryn," I began, realizing she had put me between a rock and a hard place. Spencer wanted me to be on his side, but I sort of got where she was coming from in regards to respecting the idea that people could change. "Listen, I understand what you're trying to convey, but you probably should work on your delivery."

Bryn's smile broadened as she shifted her gaze between Spencer and me. "You and Jasper are attracted to the same kind of person."

Now I was confused. Bryn pinched her thumb and forefinger together on both hands, closed her eyes, and took in a loud, deep breath. Spencer and I widened our eyes at each other as she moaned, releasing the air from her lungs.

"Sorry, Spence," she said, eyes still closed. "This is not how I pictured this going." Finally, her lids lifted, and she had a totally different look on her face—a more open one. "I didn't mean to come here and insult you at every turn. I'm better than that—at least I am now." Then she turned to me. "You must think I am totally off my rocker. And I am, or at least I was raised to be. But I'm freeing myself from that, and I'm so glad you're here while my brother is doing the same." She swept her attention back to Spencer. "And shit, we're freed Christmases. And by the way, your girl is lovely, Spence."

The way she said it left me pondering where she'd gotten that phrase.

"Bryn," Spencer said, glaring at her with laser focus. "What do you want? And why are you here?" He shook his head briskly. "And you never answered how in the hell you found me in the first place."

She spread her hand on her chest. "And that's your response to me baring my soul?"

"I've heard your words. But your actions say something different."

Bryn shook her head. "There's nothing I can do, is there, Spence?" Her voice cracked.

"Yeah. You can call before you come."

"I tried," she blared, her voice echoing in the room. "I've been sending you emails for almost a year. I miss you. I love you. I'm your sister."

I sat immobilized, feeling every bit of her plea for her brother's love. But Spencer only stared at her as if searching for something deep inside her, something he couldn't find. I shifted uncomfortably in my seat, wanting to get involved and be a mediator between the two of them but knowing that it behooved me to stay out of their family business. Plus, I was still trying to place Bryn's quote.

"Listen, Spence," she finally said, taking the extreme emotion out of her voice. "I'm hosting a real Christmas dinner at the Christmas mansion this year. Why don't you come?"

Spencer's glare gave way to a boisterous laugh. "Are you fucking crazy? The mansion? I'm never going back to that fucking place, and you shouldn't either."

"But you're here," Bryn said.

Spencer's laugh stopped immediately. He glanced at me as if looking right through me. When I reached out for his hand, it took him a few seconds to latch on.

"I know I'm here." He sounded as if he was restraining a wall of thunder.

Bryn's gaze roamed the room and then she hugged herself. "This place is just as creepy as that place," she whispered.

The siblings stared at each other as if silently communicating. Finally, Spencer cleared his throat. "I can't have Christmas with you." He had to clear his throat again. "I promised Jada I'd spend it with her and her family."

I worked like crazy to control my surprise, but I wasn't sure my initial widening of the eyes hadn't gone unnoticed by Bryn.

"I don't want us to keep falling apart, Spence." She sounded so sad that I almost pulled the covers off Spencer's lie. Thank goodness, at that moment the servers entered the dining room with dinner, which was puffy fried soufflé potatoes with blackened shrimp on a bed of roasted zucchini. The break in their deeply emotional conversation was a welcome blessing, especially since I could tell Spencer was digging in and not letting go.

"Your girl is lovely, Hubbell," I said, smirking at Bryn as we were all served and the wine was being poured.

Her eyes smiled more than her lips. "*The Way We Were*."

"But I'm nothing like Hubbell's new girl."

Spencer watched our interaction like an eagle.

She sniffed. "In relation to the women in Spence's past, you are."

I grunted thoughtfully as, once again, Carol popped into my mind. "So, Bryn, what do you do for a living?"

Her smile wavered. "I'm in between professions."

"You're out of the movie business?" Spencer asked.

She took a deep breath and picked up her knife and fork. "It seems our rendition of the Christmases' story couldn't compete with Holly's." She narrowed her eyes at me. "You've read the book, haven't you?"

I glanced at Spencer and then set my focus back on Bryn. "Yes."

"Well…" She sawed through the shrimp as if envisioning someone's head on her plate. "Holly used to be a good friend of mine, and her unforgiving rendition of me seems to be what the people want to believe. So what do you think?" She popped half a shrimp into her mouth.

"What do I think?" I asked, needing clari-fication.

"Yes, about the book. What do you think?"

I paused and then shrugged indifferently. "Most families have deep dark secrets."

Bryn grunted as she raised her eyebrows. "Are you confessing something about the great Patricia Forte?"

I let out a snort of dismissive laughter. "Oh, no. My family's the opposite. We tell each other too much shit."

"Humph," Spencer grunted and continued eating.

"By the way, Jada, your mother is how I found Spencer," Bryn said.

My mouth dropped. "What?"

She explained how my mother had gotten in contact with her after having my phone call traced to a cell tower near the ranch. Somehow, my mom had gotten Jasper Christmas's name through the transfer of cash into my banking account, which had been made by Pete Sykes. She first contacted Jasper but hit a brick wall when he wouldn't take her calls, even when she tried to throw her weight around.

"Then she called me. When she mentioned

Spencer and Jackson Hole, Wyoming, I put one and one together and came up with this place." Her gaze rolled around the room in the same way it had earlier. "I don't know why you bought the ranch and why you're here. But I bet there's a reason, and it's a good one." She looked at Spencer as if expecting him to ease her curiosity.

I had to force the tension out of my lips. "That sounds like my mother."

"Yeah?" Bryn said, sounding highly inquisitive. "She's creepily controlling, then."

I snorted. "Very."

She raised her eyebrows. "And you don't know why?"

I shrugged, annoyed by her question. "Because she's a mother."

"No," she said, shaking her head adamantly. "Not all mothers are that pathologically controlling. Only the ones who need to be."

It felt as if cement raced through my body, collecting in my brain, which made it very hard to process what she was alluding to. I continued to eat in silence, allowing the icky feelings stirring inside me to resolve as Bryn continued her plea for Spencer to allow her to be in his life more than he had recently.

"Neither of us ever see Jasper anymore. He's married to Holly and has his brand-new family, and we're only a second thought to him."

"That's not true," Spencer said.

"You say that because you're fine with being lonely." Bryn slapped herself on the chest. "I'm not. And, Jada…" she said, making me sit up straight. "That's the thing about having brothers, right?"

I jerked my neck. "I don't have a brother. I'm an only child."

"Oh," she said, surprised, and narrowed her eyes at Spencer. "I see."

I sat up straight. "You see what?"

"I just thought…" She pushed a hand toward me dismissively. "Never mind."

"If I had a brother, then I would tell you, but I don't," I said, feeling as if I had to defend myself.

"I just… maybe I got you mixed up with another one of my brother's girlfriends. Have you heard from Ash?" she asked, looking at Spencer.

They continued a conversation about Bryn's twin and how she felt he'd fallen deeper into despair. Again, Spencer disagreed with her. I listened to them, stewing in my own discomfort and mild anger. I didn't like Bryn's attempt to converse about my family and all the false insinuations she'd made. Sure, my mother was controlling, but to insinuate that she was because she had secrets was just not true. I'd been intrigued by Bryn and thought I liked her, but suddenly, I wasn't so sure. There was something inherently cruel about her. She talked as if she didn't understand the things she said, but I knew her words had been carefully crafted and spoken with intent.

I remained virtually silent for the rest of dinner, smiling on cue. She was having a high time discussing Asher's misfortune. Apparently, the woman he used to be involved with was a hooker. Bryn had to point out that if I'd gotten far enough in the book, I would have known that. I showed her my phony smile. Then she went on to say they had broken up and Asher had fallen off the face of the earth.

"You really haven't heard from him either?" she said.

"If I had, I would tell you," Spencer said.

She grunted thoughtfully. "Well, I'll find him before Christmas, come hell or high water. My next step is New York." She tapped the tips of her fingers on the table nervously. "I'm going to see Jasper and Holly and baby Jane. Have you met your niece yet?" She watched Spencer as if she already knew the answer to the question.

He shrugged. "Not yet."

"Okay, then." Bryn sprang to her feet. "I'm leaving."

Spencer seemed surprised, and he stood as well. "Okay."

"Now…" She tossed the cloth napkin that was in her lap on top of her plate. "Don't be a stranger, Spence. And stop ignoring my emails." She winked at me as if she knew I was the one answering them. "Nice meeting you, Holly." She slapped a hand over her mouth. Then, lowering her hand, she smirked cynically. "Oh, I meant *Jada*. Spencer always wanted one of her of his own, and here you are."

Spencer shook his head, sneering at Bryn as she turned her back on us and walked out of the dining room—and our lives—just as fast as she'd appeared.

CHAPTER TWENTY

JADA FORTE

After Bryn left, Spencer and I went to my bedroom. It took him no time to brush his teeth, strip down to nothing, and crawl into bed. I couldn't get the anxious feeling out of me as, still in my skirt and bra, I stood at the sink, scrubbing my face. I had just told Spencer that I didn't like what his sister was suggesting about my mom.

"She didn't mean anything by it," he said.

I rolled my eyes at my image in the mirror. I could hardly believe he was defending her, seeing as she'd spent the first part of dinner needling him. "And what was this?" I dropped my face towel on the sink and pressed my forefingers and thumbs together, imitating what Bryn had done when she decided to stop being mean to her brother and start screwing with me instead.

"What was what?" he said from the bed.

I stormed out from in front of the vanity to show him what I was doing.

Spencer laughed his head off, but I just shook mine. "It's not funny, Spencer. She's destructive."

"I thought you were into Bryn for a moment."

I shook my head rapidly. "'Into Bryn'? What does that mean?"

He smirked, and for once, I was too inflamed to want to kiss him for it. "Most women like Bryn's brand of female."

I felt my face squish into a frown. "What's Bryn's brand of female?"

"She's unrestrained. Most women are buttoned up, living by rules and shit. Bryn's is the antithesis of that. That's all I'm saying."

I cocked my head, absorbing everything he'd just said. "Did you just say *antithesis*?"

Spencer's eyebrows pulled. "Did I?"

I could feel my smile smolder. "Yes, you did. It was hot, by the way."

"Then you like clever men?"

"Very much," I purred to my surprise. I didn't even recognize my own voice.

"Damn, I wish I could think of some more words that'll get your ass over here on this bed already."

I quickly turned to glance over my shoulder. The water was still running in the sink, and my face was still damp but not as moist as what was between my legs.

Spencer's eyes narrowed to a lustful haze. "Come here, Jada."

My heart thumped like an overheated radiator. "The water," I barely said.

"Leave it." He held out a hand. "Come here."

Each step was slow as my conscience pulled me to do what I thought was right—turn off the water. Meanwhile, my desire tugged me toward what I wanted—Spencer all over me.

I gave myself to him completely when I got close enough, and he drew me onto the bed. He rolled me onto my back. Spencer unbuttoned the side of my skirt then slid down the short zipper, undressing me as if I were his sacred artifact.

"Your ass looked delectable in this skirt," he said, taking my garment by the hem and sliding it down my legs.

"Um, delectable," I hummed seductively.

"Don't move," he said as I twisted my bum to make it easier.

I didn't move a muscle as his fingers snaked under the crotch of my wet panties and plunged in and out of my wet pussy. With his other hand, he unclipped my bra between my breasts, setting them free. He watched them, sucking air between his teeth. I moaned and writhed as he never eased the speed of finger-fucking me while his warm mouth covered my nipple. His tongue rounded the hardness, and his teeth scraped the tip. The sensations sent me reeling and lifting my chest and hips to give him more. At the same time, I was in such a pleasure overload that I wanted to pull away to give myself a reprieve.

"Be still," he commanded after his mouth abandoned one of my breasts to pay the same attention to the other.

I closed my eyes, trying to not move an inch.

"Um…" he said with one last hard suck and nibble on my nipple.

I jerked from the stinging and gasped.

"Good girl…" Spencer curled his hands under my thighs, and after one smooth maneuver, he was standing on the side of the bed, pumping his cock in and out of my pussy. "Fuck," he muttered, not missing a beat.

My head rolled above my neck then jerked back and forth. I could feel every inch of him as I called out his name.

"Damn it," he said, increasing his pace. Then he tossed his head back as his condom restrained his warm wetness.

Our hazy gazes connected, basking in the after-glow of what we had just done. He stood between my legs, and I positioned myself on my arms. We refused to look away from each other. The longer we stayed in that pose, the more I wanted to know what he was thinking. The seconds mounted. I dared not ask.

Finally, Spencer pulled himself out of me. "Be still. Don't move."

His absence had released me from whatever trance our eye contact had put me in. I remained very still as he walked to the bathroom. My legs were still parted and pussy still weeping for more of him when I heard the water turn off in the vanity area. Our gazes connected again when he returned with a warm towel and wiped my pussy then threw the washcloth over his shoulder, pushed me toward the headboard, and spread my thighs as far as they could go before sucking my oversensitive clit into his mouth.

———

"Ah!" I screamed at the top of my lungs, twisting my body to bear the orgasm racing through my pussy. He had made me come seven times already and was now kissing his way up my stomach, sinking his tongue into my belly button, then squeezing my tits while his mouth consumed mine. Spencer and I rolled around on the bed, kissing deeply and passionately as if we'd die if we stopped.

"Oh, baby, I…" he whispered, squeezing me so tightly that I felt as if our bodies would merge into one.

"What?" I whispered, cheek-to-cheek with him as my fingers slid through his soft hair.

Spencer shifted me onto my side, pressing my back against his front. His breaths came heavy against my ears as he groped every part of my tits. I put my hands over his, going along for the ride. It was clear it would take a long time before Spencer and I got each other out of our systems. When I turned to face him, his mouth melted against mine, and I was soon on my back again, kissing feverishly.

His mouth went to my pussy. Then he was inside me again, this time making love to me with slow, deep thrusts. By the way he moaned and whimpered, I could tell he felt every bit of me just as I had him.

———

THE STAFF WERE NOW USED TO SEEING US IN BED together, and I was used to them seeing us this way, which was why I didn't flinch when the servers, Ignacio and Ray, rolled breakfast in on a cart. I lay facing away from the action, covers pulled up to my neck, relishing the scent of French toast, scrambled eggs, fried potatoes, and bacon, which I'd requested earlier in a sleepy haze, when Spencer asked what I wanted for breakfast.

"Thanks, Ignacio," Spencer said.

"You're welcome, Mr. Christmas."

I heard their steps rushing past my bed, and then the door closed behind them. Finally, we were alone. With a bright morning smile fueled by total satisfaction, I turned around.

"Oh," I said, surprised.

Spencer was dressed in his dusty camouflage

pants and a black sweatshirt, the shirt collar beneath it rising around his neck.

"It's been a good break, but I have to get back to it," he said.

I still wanted more of him around me, beside me, inside me. I frowned, irritated that he was choosing his mysterious project over morning sex. "What are you looking for down there, anyway?"

He tilted his head, his eyes scolding me. "You already know the answer to that, babe."

I sighed, remembering I'd agreed not to ask him about what he was doing beneath the house after he promised he wasn't engaging in illegal activity.

"Wow," I said, letting it go. I twisted my body seductively, pushing out my tits so he could get an eyeful.

Spencer narrowed an eye, focusing intently on my face. "Wow what?"

"You called me 'babe' so easily," I replied, simpering.

He smirked naughtily and thumbed over his shoulder. "I've got to go." His gaze relished my nakedness and then rested solidly on my face. "Enjoy breakfast, and don't work too hard."

"You either."

He winked at me and headed toward the bathroom. Boldly, he opened the entrance to his secret world and closed himself inside it. Once I was alone, I had to have an answer to the question that was aggravating me. I got up, walked to the mirror, and tried pulling it open.

"Damn it."

It was locked.

AS I ATE BREAKFAST, BASKING IN THE exhilaration of three straight days of making beautiful love to Spencer, I took my phone out of airplane mode and allowed my fingers to dial up Mother.

"Jada," she said, answering on the first ring.

"Hey, Mom."

"I've been trying to call you."

"Sorry, I was away from my phone."

"You're working for Spencer Christmas?" Her tone was laced with accusation.

"Yes. And, um, he's going to be joining us for the dinner party."

A deathly silence fell between us as I waited for her next response.

"Why is your boss accompanying you to

Christmas Eve dinner?" she finally asked in an overly formal tone.

I pressed my lips together, remembering how Bryn had made me feel about my mother during her short visit. I found myself questioning my mom's line of questioning. I wanted her to ask if there was something more going on between Spencer and me, but instead, she kept him in the role she would be comfortable with—to her, he was my boss.

"He's not only my boss, Mom. We're together."

"Is that so? How old is he? I was picturing someone a lot younger for you—someone not so worldly, if you know what I mean."

I knew what she meant. She was referring to the Spencer Christmas depicted in the book.

"I'm not a child, Mother. I live alone in New York City."

"How old is he?" she snapped as if what I'd just said hadn't sunk in.

"I don't know. I don't care. But he's not that much older than I am."

"Jim Lovell will be joining us for dinner. I wanted you to get to know him. He has a job for you in public relations. You'll be managing him and his campaign and not working as an assistant." She said *assistant* as if it was a dirty word.

I bent over, covering my face with a hand. "Mom, I already have a job."

"Ha." Her disapproval blared loudly in just that one little word. "Well, I guess I can't change your mind. Bring him."

I twisted my mouth, contemplating what to say next. Whenever Patricia Forte gave up that easily, there was a catch-22. I briefly considered letting Spencer know we should take Bryn up on her invitation, but just thinking of putting up with her passive-aggressive behavior made my stomach uneasy. Since the relationship between Spencer and me was fresh and new, and I didn't want anyone to knock us off course, I took a risk and decided to go with the devil I knew.

"All right, then, we'll see you on Christmas Eve for dinner."

"All right," my mom said with more than a reasonable level of irritation. "I have to go."

"Me too."

She ended the call without saying goodbye, therefore fucking with my head once again. I sat still in the chair for a long time, wondering if I should see my own version of Spencer's Dr. Mita Sharma.

No one could get to me like my mother, and at some point in my adult life, that really should have stopped being the case. Patricia had a way of making me feel like an insolent child, and that moment, I hated her for it just as much as I loved her.

I groaned and mussed up my hair, agitating my scalp. I decided to stop thinking about my mother and get to work. One deep sigh propelled me to my feet. I went into the bathroom to shower, half hoping Spencer would join me. The other part of me felt the loads of fucking we'd been doing. My body ached as though I'd lifted weights for three days straight. Spencer was an active lover, flipping me this way and that, contorting me on one side and the other. I loved watching his engorged cock go in and out of my mound, stroking my pussy in all sorts of positions.

I'd been in the shower a while, taking my time washing my hair and body, when it became clear that Spencer wouldn't be joining me. I turned off the water, dried off, and readied myself for the office.

Later that day, I was in a finance-and-planning meeting with all the department heads, including Carol. I kept watching her, seeing if she noticed the change in me. However, she was careful to not make eye contact with me, so after a while, I focused on taking accurate notes for Spencer and writing down specific questions the officers of his company had for him.

Once again, my day blew by with more meetings, more documents to sign, and more requests for Spencer to appear in person. Spencer joined me for dinner. His mood seemed heavy, but he attentively listened as I told him the high points of the day's meetings and described my mother's reaction to the news about him joining us for Christmas Eve dinner.

He stroked his chin as he frowned thoughtfully. "Jimmy Lovell, huh?"

I shrugged. "I've never heard of him. Have you?"

"Yes."

I waited for him to elaborate. "Are you going to tell me how you know him?"

"He's a wannabe politician from my home state."

"Rhode Island." I grunted thoughtfully. My mom often groomed politicians from other states so they could eventually become her political allies in

Congress. She was shrewd that way and said it was all part of effective politics.

He watched me with that indecipherable expression of his and then sat up straight, smirking. "I missed you today."

I beamed. "I missed you too."

His smirk turned naughty. "Let's finish dinner so I can eat you too."

I ate the last bite of my risotto and said I was ready to go to the bedroom. Spencer wasted no time pushing his chair back, getting up, taking my hand, and leading me upstairs.

CHAPTER TWENTY-ONE

SPENCER CHRISTMAS

J ada didn't know that every waking moment, I had been riddled by anxiety. The next day was Christmas Eve, and I felt as if I were getting closer to discovering what I was looking for. My jackhammer blasted through the concrete like an explosion. This was it. If I found nothing here, then there was nothing to be found on the ranch. That would mean I had heard wrong.

I stopped to catch my breath. As I pulled the shield from over my face and swiped the sweat off my forehead, I recalled that conversation I'd heard between my father and Arthur Valentine. I was thirteen, maybe fourteen. It was after Amelia had told me the truth. I remembered everything they'd said —at least I thought I did.

"They're at the ranch," my father said.

"Fuck, Randolph," Arthur muttered. "Where did you put the bodies?"

"They'll never find them."

"Where?" Arthur insisted.

"Don't worry about it."

"Fucking where?" Arthur roared.

I quickly hid in the secret vestibule outside the room they were in. As a kid, I liked roaming the house, searching. I didn't know what I was looking for until the day I heard the conversation between my father and Valentine.

"They're buried. In concrete. At the ranch," my father said.

"Shit." Arthur sighed. "Who?"

"I think one of the kids' mothers. Petrov's there too. I had Petrov specially handled."

Valentine grunted, then my father said he had some fun for him upstairs.

"I like the sound of that," Arthur said. Then the door opened and closed.

I put my face mask back on, lifted my jackhammer, and pressed the tip against the concrete. I bought the ranch a year and a half ago. It wasn't for sale. I had to convince the owner to sell it to me, which meant I paid four times what it was worth. For one year, I led a crew of professional excavators to search every inch of the property, using top-of-the-line technology. No mass graves were found. The team kept asking questions that I didn't want to answer, so I decided to pay them and let them go. They'd each signed a nondisclosure agreement. Plus, due to the nature of their business, I never feared any of them would talk to the press. Searching with discretion was what they did, but at some point, they thought I was crazy as hell for making them comb parts of the property they knew would turn up no results.

While they worked outside, I worked the tunnels with Gabe, the architect I'd hired to read the secret blueprint I'd found—the one my father hadn't submitted to the county when he built the structures of the ranch. Gabe tagged all the walls in the caves that were not load bearing. Once I knew where to break concrete, I paid him and sent him away. I turned on my jackhammer and chiseled away at the last area that could yield results. Before Jada arrived, I worked at this night and day. I barely slept or ate, and I never thought I wanted to fuck again. My dick had had enough.

The metal pounded the concrete, and I suddenly caught sight of white fragments mixed with gray dust. My chest grew tight as I put my tool on low-power mode and chiseled carefully around what looked like a bone. And then…

"Shit," I muttered. I'd found what I was looking for.

I exposed more white. My arms grew weak. I turned off the jackhammer before it fell out of my hands, and I dropped to my knees.

"Fuck!" Then I hung my head, feeling as if all the life had been drained out of me, and whispered, "Fuck."

Get *Impulse*, book two of **The Freed Billionaire Spencer Christmas Trilogy** now!

Made in the USA
San Bernardino, CA
16 June 2020